"What are you afraid of?"

"Afraid of?" she echoed unsteadily. "I'm not afraid of anything!" She took a deep, shuddering breath. "We have nothing to talk about."

"I forsee a long day ahead of us," Luc commented.

Catherine bent her head. "I don't have to answer your questions," she said tightly, struggling to keep a dismaying tremor out of her voice. Fight fire with fire. That was the only stance to take with Luc.

"Think of it as a small and somewhat belated piece of civility," Luc advised. "Four and a half years ago, you vanished into thin air. Without a word, a letter or a hint of explanation. I would like that explanation now."

LYNNE GRAHAM was born in Ireland and, at the age of fifteen, submitted her first romantic novel, unsuccessfully. Just when she was planning a career, a Christmas visit home resulted in her having to make a choice between career or marriage to a man she had loved since her teens. They live in Ireland in a household overflowing with dogs, plants and books. When their daughter was a toddler, Lynne began writing again, this time with success.

Books by Lynne Graham

HARLEQUIN PRESENTS

LYNNE GRAHAM

Tempestuous Reunion

Harlequin Books

TORONTO • NEW YORK • LONDON
AMSTERDAM • PARIS • SYDNEY • HAMBURG
STOCKHOLM • ATHENS • TOKYO • MILAN
MADRID • WARSAW • BUDAPEST • AUCKLAND

Harlequin Presents first edition May 1993
ISBN 0-373-11551-2

Original hardcover edition published in 1991
by Mills & Boon Limited

TEMPESTUOUS REUNION

CHAPTER ONE

'MARRY you?' Luc echoed, his brilliant dark gaze rampant with incredulity as he abruptly cast aside the financial report he had been studying. 'Why would I want to marry you?'

Catherine's slender hand was shaking. Hurriedly she set down her coffee-cup, her courage sinking fast. 'I just wondered if you had ever thought of it.' Her restless fingers made a minute adjustment to the siting of the sugar bowl. She was afraid to meet his eyes. 'It was just an idea.'

'Whose idea?' he prompted softly. 'You are perfectly content as you are.'

She didn't want to think about what Luc had made of her. But certainly contentment had rarely featured in her responses. From the beginning she had loved him wildly, recklessly, and with that edge of desperation which prevented her from ever standing as his equal.

Over the past two years, she had swung between ecstasy and despair more times than he would ever have believed. Or cared to believe. This beautiful, luxurious apartment was her prison. Not his. She was a pretty songbird in a gilded cage for Luc's exclusive enjoyment. But it wasn't bars that kept her imprisoned, it was love.

She stole a nervous glance at him. His light intonation had been deceptive. Luc was silently seething. But not at her. His ire was directed at some imaginary scapegoat, who had dared to contaminate her with ideas, quite embarrassing ideas above her station.

'Catherine,' he pressed impatiently.

Under the table the fingernails of her other hand grooved sharp crescents into her damp palm. Skating on thin ice wasn't a habit of hers with Luc. 'It was my own idea and . . . I'd appreciate an answer,' she dared in an ironic lie, for she didn't really want that answer; she didn't want to hear it.

Had the Santini electronics empire crashed overnight, Luc could not have looked more grim than he did now, pierced by a thorn from a normally very well-trained source. 'You have neither the background nor the education that I would require in my wife. There, it is said,' he delivered with the decisive speed and the ruthlessness which had made his name as much feared as respected in the business world. 'Now you need wonder no longer.'

Every scrap of colour slowly drained from her cheeks. She recoiled from the brutal candour she had invited, ashamed to discover that she had, after all, nurtured a tiny, fragile hope that deep down inside he might feel differently. Her soft blue eyes flinched from his, her head bowing. 'No, I won't need to wonder,' she managed half under her breath.

Having devastated her, he relented infinitesimally. 'This isn't what I would term breakfast conversation,' he murmured with a teasing harshness that she easily translated into a rebuke for her presumption in daring to raise the subject. 'Why should you aspire to a relationship within which you would not be at ease . . . hmm? As a lover, I imagine, I am far less demanding than I would be as a husband.'

In the midst of what she deemed to be the most agonising dénouement of her life, an hysterical giggle feathered dangerously in her convulsed throat. A blunt, sun-browned finger languorously played over the knuckles showing white beneath the skin of her clenched hand. Even though she was conscious that Luc was using his customary methods of distraction, the electricity of a powerful sexual chemistry tautened her every sinew and the fleeting desire to laugh away the ashes of painful disillusionment vanished.

With a faint sigh, he shrugged back a pristine silk shirt cuff to consult the rapier-thin Cartier watch on his wrist and frowned.

'You'll be late for your meeting.' She said it for him as she stood up, for the very first time fiercely glad to see the approach of the departure which usually tore her apart.

Luc rose fluidly upright to regard her narrowly. 'You're jumpy this morning. Is there something wrong?'

The other matter, she registered in disbelief, was already forgotten, written off as some impulsive and foolishly feminine piece of nonsense. It wouldn't occur to Luc that she had deliberately saved that question until he was about to leave. She hadn't wanted to spoil the last few hours they would ever spend together.

'No... what could be wrong?' Turning aside, she reddened. But he had taught her the art of lies and evasions, could only blame himself when he realised what a monster he had created.

'I don't believe that. You didn't sleep last night.'

She froze into shocked stillness. He strolled back across the room to link confident arms round her small, slim figure, easing her round to face him. 'Perhaps it is your security that you are concerned about.'

The hard bones and musculature of the lean, superbly fit body against hers melted her with a languor she couldn't fight. And, arrogantly acquainted with that shivery weakness, Luc was satisfied and soothed. A long finger traced the tremulous fullness of her lower lip. 'Some day our paths will separate,' he forecast in a roughened undertone. 'But that day is still far from my mind.'

Dear God, did he know what he did to her when he said things like that? If he did, why should he care? In probably much the same fashion he cracked the whip over key executives to keep them on their toes. He was murmuring something smooth about stocks and shares that she refused to listen to. You can't buy love, Luc. You can't pay for it either. When are you going to find that out?

While his hunger for her remained undiminished, she understood that she was safe. She took no compliment from the desire she had once naïvely believed was based on emotion. For the several days a month which Luc allotted cool-headedly to the pursuit of light entertainment, she had every attention. But that Luc had not even guessed that the past weeks had been unadulterated hell for her proved the shallowness of the bond on his side. She had emerged from the soap-bubble fantasy she had started building against reality two years ago. He didn't love her. He hadn't suddenly woken up one day to realise that he couldn't live without her...and he never would.

'You'll be late,' she whispered tautly, disconcerted by the glitter of gold now burnishing the night-dark scrutiny skimming her upturned face. When Luc decided to leave, he didn't usually linger.

The supple fingers resting against her spine pressed her closer, his other hand lifting to wind with cool possessiveness into the curling golden hair tumbling down her back. *'Bella mia,'* he rhymed in husky Italian, bending his dark head to taste her moistly parted lips with the inherent sensuality and the tormenting expertise which all along had proved her downfall.

Stabbed by her guilty conscience, she dragged herself fearfully free before he could taste the strange, unresponsive chill that was spreading through her. 'I'm not feeling well,' she muttered in jerky excuse, terrified that she was giving herself away.

'Why didn't you tell me that sooner? You ought to lie down.' He swept her up easily in his arms, started to kiss her again, and then, with an almost imperceptible darkening of colour, abstained long enough to carry her into the bedroom and settle her down on the tossed bed.

He hovered, betraying a rare discomfiture. Scrutinising her wan cheeks and the pared-down fragility of her bone-structure, he expelled his breath in a sudden sound of derision. 'If this is another result of one of those asinine diets of yours, I'm likely to lose my temper. When are you going to get it through your head that I like you as you are? Do you want to make yourself ill? I don't have any patience with this foolishness, Catherine.'

'No,' she agreed, beyond seeing any humour in his misapprehension.

'See your doctor today,' he instructed. 'And if you don't, I'll know about it. I'll mention it to Stevens on my way out.'

At the reference to the security guard, supposedly there for her protection but more often than not, she suspected, there to police her every move, she curved her cheek into the pillow. She didn't like Stevens. His deadpan detachment and extreme formality intimidated her.

'How are you getting on with him, by the way?'

'I understood that I wasn't supposed to get on with your security men. Isn't that why you transferred Sam Halston?' she muttered, grateful for the change of subject, no matter how incendiary it might be.

'He was too busy flirting with you to be effective,' Luc parried with icy emphasis.

'That's not true. He was only being friendly,' she protested.

'He wasn't hired to be friendly. If you'd treated him like an employee he'd still be here,' Luc underlined with honeyed dismissal. 'And now I really have to leave. I'll call you from Milan.'

He made it sound as if he were dispensing a very special favour. In fact, he called her every day no matter where he was in the world. And now he was gone.

When that phone did ring tomorrow, it would ring and ring through empty rooms. For tortured minutes she just lay and stared at the space where he had been. Dark and dynamic, he was hell on wheels for a vulnerable woman. In their entire association she had never had an argument with Luc. By fair means or foul, Luc always got his own way. Her feeble attempts to assert herself had long since sunk without trace against the tide of an infinitely more forceful personality.

He was now reputedly one of the top ten richest men in the world. At twenty-nine that was a wildly impressive achievement. He had started out with nothing but formidable intelligence in the streets of New York's Little Italy. And he would keep on climbing. Luc was always number one and never more so than in his own self-image. Power was the greatest aphrodisiac known to humanity. What Luc wanted he reached out and took, and to hell with the damage he caused as long as the backlash did not affect his comfort. And, having fought for everything he had ever got, what came easy had no intrinsic value for him.

'The lone wolf,' *Time* magazine had dubbed him in a recent article, endeavouring to penetrate the mystique of a rogue among the more conventional herd of the hugely successful.

A shark was a killing machine, superbly efficient within its own restricted field. And wolves mated for life, not for leisure-time amusement. But Luc was indeed a land-based animal and far from cold-blooded. As such he was all the more dangerous to the unwary, the innocent and the over-confident.

Technical brilliance alone hadn't built his empire. It was the energy source of one man's drive combined with a volatile degree of unpredictability which kept competitors at bay in a cut-throat market. She could have told that journalist exactly what Luc Santini was like. And that was hard, cruelly hard with the cynicism, the self-interest and the ruthless ambition that was bred into his very bones. Only a fool got in Luc's path ... only a very foolish woman could have given her heart into his keeping.

Her eyes squeezed shut on a shuddering spasm of anguish. It was over now. She would never see Luc again. No miracle had astounded her at the eleventh hour. Marriage was not, nor would it ever be, a possibility. Her small hand spread protectively over her no longer concave stomach. Luc had begun to lose her one hundred per cent loyalty and devotion from the very hour she suspected that she was carrying his child.

Instinct had warned her that the news would be greeted as a calculated betrayal and, no doubt, the conviction that she had somehow achieved the condition all on her own. Again and again she had put off telling him. In fear of discovery, she had learnt to be afraid of Luc. When he married a bride with a social pedigree, a bride bred to the lofty heights that were already his, he wouldn't want any skeletons in the cupboard. Ice-cold and sick with apprehensions that she had refused to face head on, she wiped clumsily at her swollen eyes and got up.

He would never know now and that was how it had to be. Thank God, she had persuaded Sam to show her how to work the alarm system. She would leave by the rear entrance. That would take care of Stevens. Would Luc miss her? A choked sob of pain escaped her. He

would be outraged that she could leave him and he had
not foreseen the event. But he wouldn't have any trouble
replacing her. She was not so special and she wasn't
beautiful. She never had grasped what it was about her
which had drawn Luc. Unless it was the cold intuition
of a predator scenting good doormat material downwind,
she conceded shamefacedly.

How could she be sorry to leave this half-life behind?
She had no friends. When discretion was demanded,
friends were impossible. Luc had slowly but surely isolated her so that her entire existence revolved round him.
Sometimes she was so lonely that she talked out loud to
herself. Love was a fearsome emotion, she thought with
a convulsive shudder. At eighteen she had been green as
grass. Two years on, she didn't feel she was much
brighter but she didn't build castles in the air any more.

'*Arrivederci*, Luc, *grazie tanto*,' she scrawled in lip-
stick across the mirror. A theatrical gesture, the ubiqui-
tous note. He could do without the ego boost of five
tear-stained pages telling him pointlessly that nobody was
ever likely to love him as much as she did.

Luc, she had learnt by destructive degrees, didn't rate
love any too highly. But he had not been above using
her love as a weapon against her, twisting her emotions
with cruel expertise until they had become the bars of
her prison cell.

'What are you doing with my books?'

Catherine straightened from the cardboard box and
clashed with stormy dark eyes. 'I'm packing them. Do
you want to help?' she prompted hopefully. 'We could
talk.'

Daniel kicked at a chair leg, his small body stiff and
defensive. 'I don't want to talk about moving.'

'Ignoring it isn't going to stop it happening,' Catherine
warned.

Daniel kicked moodily at the chair leg again, hands stuck in his pockets, miniature-tough style. Slowly Catherine counted to ten. Much more of this and she would scream until the little men in the white coats came to take her away. How much longer was her son going to treat her as the wickedest and worst mother in the world? With a determined smile, she said, 'Things aren't half as bad as you seem to think they are.'

Daniel looked at her dubiously. 'Have we got any money?'

Taken aback by the demand, Catherine coloured and shifted uncomfortably. 'What's that got to do with anything?'

'I heard John's mum telling Mrs Withers that we had no money 'cos if we had we would've bought this house and stayed here.'

Catherine could happily have strangled the woman for speaking so freely in Daniel's presence. He might be only four but he was precociously bright for his age. Daniel already understood far too much of what went on around him.

'It's not fair that someone can take our house off us and sell it to someone else when we want to live here forever!' he burst out without warning.

The pain she glimpsed in his over-bright eyes tore cruelly at her. Unfortunately there was little that she could do to assuage that pain. 'Greyfriars has never been ours,' she reminded him tautly. 'You know that, Daniel. It belonged to Harriet, and on her death she gave it to charity. Now the people who run that charity want to sell and use the money to——'

Daniel threw her a sudden seething glance. 'I don't care about those people starving in Africa! This is our house! Where are we going to live?'

'Drew has found us a flat in London,' she told him yet again.

'You can't keep a donkey in London!' Daniel launched at her fierily. 'Why can't we live with Peggy? She said we could.'

Catherine sighed. 'Peggy really doesn't have enough room for us.'

'I'll run away and you can live in London all on your own because I'm not going without Clover!' Daniel shouted at her in a tempestuous surge of fury and distress. 'It's all your fault. If I'd had a daddy, he could've bought us this house like everybody else's daddy does! I bet he could even have made Harriet well again... I hate you 'cos you can't do anything!'

With that bitter condemnation, Daniel hurtled out of the back door. He would take refuge in one of his hiding places in the garden. There he would sit, brooding and struggling to cope with harsh adult realities that entailed the loss of all he held dear. She touched the solicitor's letter on the table. She would be even more popular when he realised that their holiday on Peggy's family farm was no longer possible either.

Sometimes—such as now—Catherine had this engulfing sense of total inadequacy in Daniel's radius. Daniel was not quite like other children. At two he had taken apart a radio and put it back together again, repairing it in the process. At three he had taught himself German by listening to a language programme on television. But he was still too young to accept necessary sacrifices. Harriet's death had hit him hard, and now he was losing his home, a much-loved pet donkey, the friends he played with... in short, all the remaining security that had bounded his life to date. Was it any wonder that he was frightened? How could she reassure him when she too was afraid of the future?

The conviction that catastrophe was only waiting to pounce round the next blind corner had never really left Catherine. Harriet's sudden death had fulfilled her worst imaginings. With one savage blow, the tranquil and happy security of their lives had been shattered. And right now it felt as though she'd been cruelly catapulted back to where she had started out over four years ago...

Her life had been in a mess, heading downhill at a seemingly breakneck pace. She had had the promising future of a kamikaze pilot. And then Harriet had come along. Harriet, so undervalued by those who knew her best. Harriet...in his exasperation, Drew had once called her a 'charming mental deficient'. Yet Harriet had picked Catherine up, dusted her down and set her back on the rails again. In the process, Harriet had also become the closest thing to a mother that Catherine had ever known.

They had met on a train. That journey and that meeting had forever altered Catherine's future. While they had shared the same compartment, Harriet had tried repeatedly to strike up a conversation. When you were locked up tight and terrified of breaking down in public, you didn't want to talk. But Harriet's persistence had forced her out of her self-absorption, and before very long her over-taxed emotions had betrayed her and somehow she had ended up telling Harriet her life-story.

Afterwards she had been embarrassed, frankly eager to escape the older woman's company. They had left the train at the same station. Nothing poor Harriet had said about her 'having made the right decision' had penetrated. Like an addict, sick for a long-overdue fix, Catherine had been unbelievably desperate just to hear the sound of a man's voice on the phone. Throwing Harriet a guilty goodbye, she had raced off towards the phone-box she could see across the busy car park.

What would have happened had she made that call? That call that would have been a crowning and unforgivable mistake in a relationship which had been a disaster from start to finish?

She would never know now. In her mad haste to reach
that phone, she had run in front of a car. It had taken
total physical incapacitation to finally bring her to her
senses. She had spent the following three months recovering from her injuries in hospital. Days had passed
before she had been strong enough to recognise the
soothing voice that drifted in and out of her haze of
pain and disorientation. It had belonged to Harriet.
Knowing that she had no family, Harriet had sat by her
in Intensive Care, talking back the dark for her. If
Harriet hadn't been there, Catherine didn't believe she
would ever have emerged from the dark again.

Even before his premature birth, Daniel had had to
fight for survival. Coming into the world, he had
screeched for attention, tiny and weak but indomitably
strong-willed. From his incubator he had charmed the
entire medical staff by surmounting every set-back within
record time. Catherine had begun to appreciate then that,
with the genes her son carried to such an unmistakably
marked degree, a ten-ton truck couldn't have deprived
him of existence, never mind his careless mother's col-
lision with a mere car.

'He's a splendid little fighter,' Harriet had proclaimed
proudly, relishing the role of surrogate granny as only
an intensely lonely woman could. Drew had been sincerely fond of his older sister but her eccentricities had
infuriated him, and his sophisticated French wife,
Annette, and their teenage children had had no time for
Harriet at all. Greyfriars was situated on the outskirts
of an Oxfordshire village, a dilapidated old house, sur-
rounded by untamed acres of wilderness garden. Harriet
and Drew had been born here and Harriet had vocifer-
ously withstood her brother's every attempt to refurbish
the house for her. Surroundings had been supremely un-
important to Harriet. Lame ducks had been Harriet's
speciality.

Catherine's shadowed gaze roamed over the homely kitchen. She had made the gingham curtains fluttering at the window, painted the battered cupboards a cheerful fire-engine red sold off cheap at the church fête. This was their home. In every sense of the word. How could she persuade Daniel that he would be as happy in a tiny city flat when she didn't believe it herself? But, dear God, that flat was their one and only option.

A light knock sounded on the back door. Without awaiting an answer, her friend Peggy Downes breezed in. A tall woman in her thirties with geometrically cut red hair, she dropped down on to the sagging settee by the range with the ease of a regular visitor. She stared in surprise at the cardboard box. 'Aren't you being a little premature with your packing? You've still got a fortnight to go.'

'We haven't.' Catherine passed over the solicitor's letter. 'It's just as well that Drew said we could use his apartment if we were stuck. We can't stay here until the end of the month and the flat won't be vacant before then.'

'Hell's teeth! They wouldn't give you that extra week?' Peggy exclaimed incredulously.

As Peggy's mobile features set into depressingly familiar lines of annoyance, Catherine turned back to the breakfast dishes, hoping that her friend wasn't about to climb back on her soap-box to decry the terms of Harriet's will and their imminent move to city life. In recent days, while exuding the best of good intentions, Peggy had been very trying and very impractical.

'We have no legal right to be here at all,' Catherine pointed out.

'But morally you have every right and I would've expected a charitable organisation to be more generous towards a single parent.' Peggy's ready temper was rising on Catherine's behalf. 'Mind you, I don't know why I'm blaming them. This whole mess is your precious Harriet's fault!'

'Peggy——'

'Sorry, but I believe in calling a spade a spade.' That was an unnecessary reminder to anyone acquainted with Peggy's caustic tongue. 'Honestly, Catherine... sometimes I think you must have been put on this earth purely to be exploited! You don't even seem to realise when people are using you! What thanks did you get for wasting four years of your life running after Harriet?'

'Harriet gave us a home when we had nowhere else to go. She had nothing to thank me for.'

'You kept this house, waited on her hand and foot and slaved over all her pet charity schemes,' Peggy condemned heatedly. 'And for all that you received board and lodging and first pick of the jumble-sale clothes! So much for charity's beginning at home!'

'Harriet was the kindest and most sincere person I've ever known,' Catherine parried tightly.

And crazy as a coot, Peggy wanted to shriek in frustration. Admittedly Harriet's many eccentricities had not appeared to grate on Catherine as they had on other, less tolerant souls. Catherine hadn't seemed to notice when Harriet talked out loud to herself and her conscience, or noisily emptied the entire contents of her purse into the church collection plate. Catherine hadn't batted an eyelash when Harriet brought dirty, smelly tramps home to tea and offered them the freedom of her home.

The trouble with Catherine was... It was a sentence Peggy often began and never managed to finish to her satisfaction. Catherine was the best friend she had ever had. She was also unfailingly kind, generous and unselfish, and that was quite an accolade from a female who thought of herself as a hardened cynic. How did you criticise someone for such sterling qualities? Unfortunately it was exactly those qualities which had put Catherine in her present predicament.

Catherine drifted along on another mental plane. Meeting those misty blue eyes in that arrestingly lovely face, Peggy was helplessly put in mind of a child cast adrift in a bewildering adult world. There was something so terrifyingly innocent about Catherine's penchant for seeing only the best in people and taking them on trust. There was something so horribly defenceless about her invariably optimistic view of the world.

She was a sucker for every sob-story that came her way and a wonderful listener. She didn't know how to say no when people asked for favours. This kitchen was rarely empty of callers, mothers in need of temporary childminders or someone to look after the cat or the dog or the dormouse while they were away. Catherine was very popular locally. If you were in a fix, she would always lend a hand. But how many returned those favours? Precious few, in Peggy's experience.

'At the very least, Harriet ought to have left you a share of her estate,' Peggy censured.

Catherine put the kettle on to boil. 'And how do you think Drew and his family would have felt about that?'

'Drew isn't short of money.'

'Huntingdon's is a small firm. He isn't a wealthy man.'

'He has a big house in Kent and an apartment in central London. If that isn't wealthy, what is?' Peggy demanded drily.

Catherine suppressed a groan. 'Business hasn't been too brisk for the firm recently. Drew has already had to sell some property he owned, and though he wouldn't admit it, he must have been disappointed by Harriet's will. As building land this place will fetch a small fortune. He could have done with a windfall.'

'And by the time the divorce comes through Annette will probably have stripped him of every remaining movable asset,' Peggy mused.

'She didn't want the divorce,' Catherine murmured.

Peggy pulled a face. 'What difference does that make? She had the affair. She was the guilty partner.'

Catherine made the tea, reflecting that it was no use looking to Peggy for tolerance on the subject of marital infidelity. Her friend was still raw from the break-up of her own marriage. But Peggy's husband had been a womaniser. Annette was scarcely a comparable case. Business worries and a pair of difficult teenagers had put the Huntingdon marriage under strain. Annette had had an affair and Drew had been devastated. Resisting her stricken pleas for a reconciliation, Drew had moved out and headed straight for his solicitor. Funny how people rarely reacted as you thought they would in a personal crisis. Catherine had believed he would forgive and forget. She had been wrong.

'I still hope they sort out their problems before it's too late,' she replied quietly.

'Why should he want to? He's only fifty... an attractive man, still in his prime...'

'I suppose he is,' Catherine allowed uncertainly. She was very fond of Harriet's brother, but she wasn't accustomed to thinking of him on those terms.

'A man who somehow can't find anything better to do than drive down here at weekends to play with Daniel,' Peggy commented with studied casualness.

Unconscious of her intent scrutiny, Catherine laughed. 'He's at a loose end without his family.'

Peggy cleared her throat. 'Has it ever occurred to you that Drew might have a more personal interest at stake here?'

Catherine surveyed her blankly.

'Oh, for goodness' sake!' Peggy groaned. 'Do I have to spell it out? His behaviour at the funeral raised more brows than mine. If you lifted anything heavier than a teacup, he was across the room like young Lochinvar! I think he's in love with you.'

'In love with me?' Catherine parroted, aghast. 'I've never heard anything so ridiculous!'

'I could be wrong.' Peggy sounded doubtful.

'Of course you're wrong!' Catherine told her with unusual vehemence, her cheeks hot with discomfiture.

'All right, calm down,' Peggy sighed. 'But I did have this little chat with him at the funeral. I asked him why he'd dug up another old lady for you to run after——'

'Mrs Anstey is his godmother!' Catherine gasped.

'And she'll see out another generation of downtrodden home-helps,' Peggy forecast grimly. 'When I ran you up to see the flat, that frozen face of hers was enough for me. I told Drew that.'

'Peggy, how could you? I only have to do her shopping and supply her with a main meal every evening. That isn't much in exchange for a flat at a peppercorn rent.'

'That's why I smell a big fat rat. However...' Peggy paused smugly for effect '...Drew told me that I didn't need to worry because he didn't expect you to be there for long. Now why do you think he said that?'

'Maybe he doesn't think I'll suit her.' Thank you, Peggy for giving me something else to worry about, she thought wearily.

Peggy was fingering the solicitor's letter, a crease suddenly forming between her brows. 'If you have to move this week, you can't possibly come up home with me, can you?' she gathered frustratedly. 'And I was absolutely depending on you, Catherine. My mother and you get on like a house on fire and it takes the heat off me.'

'The news isn't going to make me Daniel's favourite person either,' Catherine muttered.

Unexpectedly, Peggy grinned. 'Why don't I take him anyway?'

'On his own?'

'Why not? My parents adore him. He'll be spoilt to death. And by the time we come back you'll have the flat organised and looking more like home. I've felt so guilty about not being able to do anything to help out,' Peggy confided. 'This is perfect.'

'I couldn't possibly let you——'

'We're friends, aren't we? It would make the move less traumatic for him. Poor little beggar, he doesn't half take things to heart,' Peggy said persuasively. 'He won't be here when you hand Clover over to the animal sanctuary and he won't have to camp out *en route* in Drew's apartment either. I seem to recall he doesn't get on too well with that housekeeper.'

Daniel didn't get on too terribly well with anyone who crossed him, Catherine reflected ruefully. He especially didn't like being babied and being told that he was cute, which, regrettably for him, he was. All black curly hair and long eyelashes and huge dark eyes. He was extremely affectionate with her, but not with anyone else.

'You do trust me with him?' Peggy shot at her abruptly.

'Of course I do——'

'Well, then, it's settled,' Peggy decided with her usual impatience.

The comment that she had never been apart from Daniel before, even for a night, died on Catherine's lips. Daniel loved the farm. They had spent several weekends there with Peggy in recent years. At least this way he wouldn't miss out on his holiday.

Six days later, Daniel gave her an enthusiastic hug and raced into Peggy's car. Catherine hovered. 'If he's homesick, phone me,' she urged Peggy.

'We haven't got a home any more,' Daniel reminded her. 'Africa's getting it.'

Within minutes they were gone. Catherine retreated indoors to stare at a set of suitcases and a handful of boxes through a haze of tears. Not much to show for four years. The boxes were to go into Peggy's garage. A neighbour had promised to drop them off at Drew's apartment next week. She wiped at her overflowing eyes in vexation. Daniel was only going to be away for ten days, not six months!

Drew met her off the train and steered her out to his car. He was a broadly built man with pleasant features and a quiet air of self-command. 'We'll drop your cases off at the apartment first.'

'First?' she queried.

He smiled. 'I've booked a table at the Savoy for lunch.'

'Are you celebrating something?' Catherine had lunched with Drew a dozen times in Harriet's company, but he had always taken them to his club.

'The firm's on the brink of winning a very large contract,' he divulged, not without pride. 'Unofficially, it's in the bag. I'm flying to Germany this evening. The day after tomorrow we sign on the dotted line.'

Catherine grinned. 'That's marvellous news.'

'To be frank, it's come in the nick of time. Lately, Huntingdon's has been cruising too close to the wind. But that's not all we'll be celebrating,' he told her. 'What about your move to London?'

'When will you be back from Germany?' she asked as they left his apartment again.

'Within a couple of days, but I'll check into a hotel.'

Catherine frowned. 'Why?'

Faint colour mottled his cheeks. 'When you're in the middle of a divorce you can't be too careful, Catherine. Thank God, it'll all be over next month. No doubt you think I'm being over-cautious, but I don't want anyone pointing fingers at you or associating you with the divorce.'

Catherine was squirming with embarrassment. She had gratefully accepted his offer of a temporary roof without thought of the position she might be putting him in. 'I feel terrible, Drew. I never even thought——'

'Of course you didn't. Your mind doesn't work like that.' Drew squeezed her hand comfortingly. 'Once this court business is over, we won't need to consider clacking tongues.'

She found that remark more unsettling than re-assuring, implying as it did a degree of intimacy that had never been a part of their friendship. Then she scolded herself and blamed Peggy for making her read double meanings where no doubt none existed. She had inevitably grown closer to Drew since he had separated from Annette. He had become a frequent visitor to his sister's home.

In the bar they received their menus. Catherine made an elaborate play of studying hers, although she did have great difficulty with words on a printed page. The dif-ficulty was because she was dyslexic, but she was prac-tised at concealing the handicap.

'Steak, I think.' Steak was safe. It was on every menu.

'You're a creature of habit,' Drew complained, but he smiled at her. He was the sort of man who liked things to stay the same. 'And to start?'

She played the same game with prawns.

'I might as well have ordered for you,' he teased.

Her wandering scrutiny glanced off the rear-view of a tall black-haired male passing through the foyer beyond the doorway. At accelerated speed her eyes swept back again in a double-take, only he was out of sight. Be-musedly she blinked and then told herself off for that fearful lurch of recognition, that chilled sensation enclosing her flesh.

'Take one day at a time,' Harriet had once told her. Harriet had been a great one for clichés, and four years ago she had made it sound so easy. But a day was twenty-four hours and each of them broken up into sixty minutes. How long had it been before she could go even five minutes without remembering? How long had it been since she had lain sleepless in bed, tortured by the raw strength of the emotions she was forcing herself to deny? In the end she had built a wall inside her head. Behind it she had buried two years of her life. Beyond it sometimes she still felt only half-alive...

'Something wrong?'

Meeting Drew's puzzled gaze, she gave an exaggerated shiver. 'Someone walked over my grave,' she joked, veiling her too-expressive eyes.

'Now that you're in London, we'll be able to see each other more often,' Drew remarked tensely and reached for her hand. 'What I'm trying to say, not very well, perhaps, is...I believe I'm in love with you.'

Her hand jerked, bathing them both in sherry. With a muttered apology she fumbled into her bag for a tissue, but a waiter moved forward and deftly mopped up the table. Catherine sat, frozen, wishing that she were anywhere but where she was now, with Drew looking at her expectantly.

He sighed, 'I wanted you to know how I felt.'

'I...I didn't know. I had no idea.' It was all she could think to say, hopelessly inadequate as it was.

'I thought you might have worked it out for yourself.' There was a glimmer of wry humour in his level scrutiny. 'Apparently I haven't been as obvious as I thought I was being. Catherine, don't look so stricken. I don't expect anything from you. I don't believe there is an appropriate response for an occasion like this. I've been clumsy and impatient and I'm sorry.'

'I feel that I've come between you and Annette,' she whispered guiltily.

He frowned. 'That's nonsense. It's only since I left her that I began to realise just how much I enjoyed being with you.'

'But if I hadn't been around, maybe you would have gone back to her,' she reasoned tautly. 'You're a very good friend, but I'm ...'

He covered her hand again with his. 'I'm not trying to rush you, Catherine. We've got all the time in the world,' he assured her evenly, and deftly flipped the subject, clearly registering that further discussion at that moment would be unproductive.

They were in the River Room Restaurant when she heard the voice. Dark-timbred, slightly accented, like honey drifting down her spine. Instantly her head spun on a chord of response rooted too deep even to require consideration. Her eyes widened in shock, her every sinew jerked tight. The blood pounded dizzily in her eardrums. With a trembling hand she set down her wine glass.

Luc.

Oh, God ... Luc. It had been him earlier. It was him. His carved profile, golden and vibrant as a gypsy's, was etched in bold relief against the light flooding through the window behind him. One brown hand was moving to illustrate some point to his two male companions. That terrible compulsion to stare was uncontrollable. The lean, arrogant nose, the hard slant of his high cheekbones and the piercing intensity of deep-set dark eyes, all welded into one staggeringly handsome whole.

His gleaming dark head turned slightly. He looked straight at her. No expression. No reaction. Eyes golden as the burning heart of a flame. Her ability to breathe seized up. A clock had stopped ticking somewhere. She was sentenced to immobility while every primitive sense she possessed screamed for her to get up and run and keep on running until the threat was far behind. For a moment her poise almost deserted her. For a moment she forgot that he was very unlikely to acknowledge her. For a moment she was paralysed by sheer gut-wrenching fear.

Luc broke the connection first. He signalled with a hand to one of his companions, who immediately rose from his seat with the speed of a trained lackey, inclining his head down for his master's voice.

'I've upset you,' Drew murmured. 'I should have kept quiet.'

Her lashes dropped down like a camera shutter. The clink of cutlery and the buzz of voices swam back to her again. One thing hadn't changed, she acknowledged numbly; when she looked at Luc there was nothing and nobody else in the world capable of stealing her attention. Perspiration was beading her upper lip. Luc was less than fifteen feet away. They said that when you drowned your whole life flashed before you. Oh, for the deep concealment of a pool.

'Catherine——'

Belatedly she recalled the man she had been lunching with. 'I've got a bit of a headache,' she mumbled. 'If you'll excuse me, I'll get something for it.'

Up she got, on jellied knees, undyingly grateful that she didn't have to pass Luc's table. Even so, leaving the restaurant was like walking the plank above a gathering of sharks. An unreasoning part of her was expecting a hand to fall on her shoulder at any second. Feeling physically sick, she escaped into the nearest cloakroom and ran cold water over her wrists.

Drying her hands, she touched the slender gold band on her wedding finger. Harriet's gift, Harriet's invention. Everyone but Peggy thought she was a widow. Harriet had coined and told the lie before Catherine had even left hospital. She could not have publicly branded Harriet a liar. Even so, it had gone against the grain to pose as something she wasn't, although she was ruefully aware that, without Harriet's respectable cover-story, she would not have been accepted into the community in the same way.

Her stomach was still heaving. Calm down, breathe in. Why give way to panic? With Luc in the vicinity, panic made sense, she reasoned feverishly. Luc was very unpredictable. He threw wild cards without conscience. But she couldn't stay in here forever, could she?

'I think there must be a storm in the air,' she told Drew on her return, her eyes carefully skimming neither left nor right. 'I often get a headache when the weather's about to break.'

She talked incessantly through the main course. If Drew was a little overwhelmed by her loquacity, at least he wasn't noticing that her appetite had vanished. Luc was watching her. She could feel it. She could feel the hypnotic beat of tawny gold on her profile. And she couldn't stand it. It was like Chinese water-torture. Incessant, remorseless. Anger began to gain ground on her nerves.

Luc was untouched. It was against nature that he should be untouched after the scars he had inflicted on her. There was no justice in a world where Luc continued to flourish like a particularly invasive tropical plant. Hack it down and it leapt up again, twice as big and threatening.

And yet some day...somehow...some woman had to slice beneath that armour-plating of his. It had to happen. He had to learn what it was to feel pain from

somebody. That belief was all that had protected
Catherine from burning up with bitterness. She would
picture Luc driven to his knees, Luc humanised by suffering, and then she would filter back to reality again,
unable to sustain the fantasy.

Religiously she stirred her coffee. Clockwise, anti-
clockwise, clockwise again, belatedly adding sugar. Her
mind was in turmoil, lost somewhere between the past
and the present. She was merely one more statistic on
the long Santini casualty list. It galled her to acknowledge that demeaning truth.

'I've been cut dead.' Drew planted the observation
flatly into the flow of her inconsequential chatter.

'Sorry?' she said, all at sea.

'Luc Santini. He looked right through me on the way
out.'

She was floored by the casual revelation that Drew
actually *knew* Luc. Yet why was she so surprised? Even
if he was in a much smaller category, Drew was in the
same field as Luc. Huntingdon's manufactured com-
puter components. 'Is th-that important?' she
stammered.

'It'll teach me not to get too big for my boots,' Drew
replied wryly. 'I did do some business with him once,
but that was years ago. I'm not in the Santini league
these days. Possibly he didn't remember me.'

Luc had a memory like a steel trap. He never forgot
a face. She was guiltily conscious that Luc had cut Drew
because of her presence and for no other reason. And
she wasn't foolish enough to pretend that she didn't know
who Luc was. The individual who hadn't heard of Luc
Santini was either illiterate or living in a grass hut on a
desert island.

Drew sipped at his coffee, clearly satisfied that he had simply been forgotten. 'He's a fascinating character. Think of the risks he must have taken to get where he is today.'

'Think of the body-count he must have left behind him.'

'That's a point,' Drew mused. 'To my knowledge, he's only slipped once. Let me see, it was about four... five years ago now. I don't know what happened, but he damned near lost the shirt off his back.'

Obviously he had snatched his shirt back again and, knowing Luc, he had snatched someone else's simultaneously. On that level, Luc was unashamedly basic. An eye for an eye, a tooth for a tooth, and perhaps interest into the bargain. In remembrance she stilled a shudder.

As they left the hotel, Drew said in a driven undertone, 'I've made a bloody fool of myself, haven't I?'

'Of course you haven't,' she hastened to assure him.

'Do you want a taxi?' he asked stiffly. 'I'd better get back to the office.'

'I think I'll go for a walk.' She was ashamed that she hadn't handled the situation with greater tact, but the combination of his confession and Luc, hovering on the horizon like a pirate ship, had bereft her of her wits.

'Catherine?' Before she could turn away, Drew bent down in an almost involuntary motion and crushed her parted lips briefly with his own. 'Some day soon I'm going to ask you to marry me, whether you like it or not,' he promised with recovering confidence. 'It's nearly five years since you lost your husband. You can't bury yourself with his memory forever. And I'm a persistent man.'

A second later he was gone, walking quickly in the other direction. Tears lashed her eyes fiercely. Waves of delayed reaction were rolling over her, reducing her self-control to rubble. He was such a kind man, the essence of an old-fashioned gentleman, proposing along with the first kiss. And she was a fraud, a complete fraud. She was not the woman he thought she was, still grieving for some youthful husband and a tragically short-lived marriage. Drew had her on a pedestal.

The truth would shatter him. In retrospect, it even shattered her. For two years she had been nothing better than Luc Santini's whore, in her own mind. Kept and clothed in return for her eagerness to please in his bed. Luc hadn't once confused sex with love. That mistake had been hers alone. The polite term was 'mistress'. Only rich men's mistresses tended to share the limelight. Luc had ensured that she'd remained strictly off stage. He had never succumbed to an urge to take her out and show her off. She hadn't had the poise or the glitter, never mind the background or the education. Even now, the memories were like acid burns on her flesh, wounding and hurting wherever they touched.

Choices. Life was all about choices. Sometimes the tiniest choice could raise Cain at a later date. At eighteen Catherine had made a series of choices. At least, she had *thought* she was making them; in reality, they had most of them been made for her. Love was a terrifying leveller of pride and intelligence when a woman was an insecure girl. Before she had met Luc, she wouldn't have believed that it could be a mistake to love somebody. But it could be, oh, yes, it could be. If that person turned your love into a weapon against you, it could be a mistake you would regret for the rest of your days.

From no age at all, Catherine had been desperate to be loved. With hindsight she could only equate herself with a walking time-bomb, programmed to self-destruct. Within hours of her birth, she had been abandoned by her mother and her reluctant parent had never been traced. Nor had anybody ever come forward with any information.

She had grown up in a children's home where she had been one of many. She had been a dreamer, weaving fantasies for years about the unknown mother who might eventually come to claim her. When that hope had worn thin in her teens, she had dreamt of a towering passion instead.

Leaving school at sixteen, she had worked as a helper in the home until it had closed down two years later The Goulds had been related to the matron. A young sophisticated couple, they had owned a small art gallery in London. Giving her a job as a receptionist, the Goulds had paid her barely enough to live on and had taken gross advantage of her willingness to work long hours. Business had been poor at the gallery and it had been kept open late most nights, Catherine left in charge on the many evenings that her employers went out.

Luc had strolled in one wet winter's night when she'd been about to lock up. His hotel had been near by. He had walked in off the street on impulse, an off-white trenchcoat carelessly draped round his shoulders, crystalline raindrops glistening in his luxuriant black hair and that aura of immense energy and self-assurance splintering from him in waves. She had made her first choice then, bedazzled and bemused by a fleeting smile...she had stopped locking up.

A silver limousine purred into the kerb several yards ahead of her now, penetrating her reverie. She hadn't even noticed where she'd been walking. Looking up, she found herself in a quiet side-street. The rear door of the car swung open and Luc stepped out on to the pavement, blocking her path. 'May I offer you a lift?'

CHAPTER TWO

CATHERINE focused on him in unconcealed horror, eyes wide above her pale cheeks. 'I'm . . . I'm not going anywhere——'

'You're simply loitering?' Luc gibed.

'That I would need a lift,' she completed jerkily. 'How did you know where I was?'

A beautifully shaped brown hand moved deprecatingly.

'How?' she persisted.

'I had you followed from the hotel.'

Oxygen locked in her throat. Had she really thought this second meeting a further coincidence? Had she really thought he would let her go without a single question? A car pulled up behind the limousine, two security men speedily emerging. Like efficient watchdogs, one of them took up a stance to Luc's rear, the other backing across the street for a better vantage point. For Catherine, there was an unreality to the scene. She was reminded of how vastly different a world she had inhabited over the past four years.

'Why would you want to do that?' she whispered tautly.

Black spiky lashes lowered over glittering dark eyes. 'Perhaps I wanted to catch up on old times. I don't know. You tell me,' he invited softly. 'Impulse? Do you think that is a possibility?'

Involuntarily she backed towards the railings behind her. 'You're not an impulsive person.'

'Why are you trembling?' He moved soundlessly closer, and her shoulders met wrought iron in an effort to keep the space between them intact.

'You come up out of nowhere? You gave me one heck of a fright!'

'You used to have the love of a child for surprises.'

'You might not have noticed, but I'm not a child any more!' It took courage to hurl the retort, but it was a mistake. Luc ran a raking, insolent appraisal over her, taking in the purple bullclip doing a haphazard task of holding up her silky hair, the lace-collared blouse and the tiered floral skirt cinched at her tiny waist with a belt. Modestly covered as she was, she still felt stripped.

'I see Laura Ashley is still doing a roaring trade,' he said drily.

He was so close now that she could have touched him. But she wouldn't raise her eyes above the level of his blue silk tie. He wore a dove-grey suit with an elegance few men could emulate. Superb tailoring outlined his lean length in the cloth of a civilised society. However, what she sensed in the atmosphere was far from civilised. It was nameless, frightening. A silent intimidation that clawed cruelly at her nerve-endings.

'We don't have anything to talk about after all this time.' The assurance left her bloodless lips in a rush, an answer to an unvoiced but understood demand.

Negligently he raised a hand and a fingertip roamed with taunting slowness from her delicate collarbone where a tiny pulse was flickering wildly up to the taut curve of her full lower lip. Her skin was on fire, her entire body suddenly consumed by a heatwave.

'Relax,' he cajoled, carelessly withdrawing his hand a split second before she jerked her head back in violent repudiation of the intimacy. Flames danced momentarily in his dark eyes and then a slow, brilliant smile curved his hard mouth. 'I didn't intend to frighten you. Come . . . are we enemies?'

'I'm in r . . . rather a hurry,' she stammered.

'And you still don't want a lift? Fine. I'll walk along with you,' he responded smoothly. 'Or we could get into the car and just drive around for a while . . . even sit in a traffic jam. Believe me, I'm in an unusually accommodating mood.'

'Why?' Valiantly moving away from the hard embrace of the railings, Catherine straightened her shoulders. 'What do you want?'

'Well, I don't expect you to do what we used to do in traffic jams.' Slumbrous dark eyes rested unrepentantly on the tide of hot colour spreading beneath her fair skin. 'What do you think I might want? Surely, it's understandable that I should wish to satisfy a little natural curiosity?'

'What about?'

'About you. What else?' An ebony brow quirked. 'Do you think I am standing here in the street for my own pleasure?'

Catherine chewed indecisively at her lower lip. She could feel his temper rising. Time was when Luc would have said 'get in the car' and she would have leapt. He was smiling, but you couldn't trust Luc's smiles. Luc could smile while he broke you in two with a handful of well-chosen words. Without speaking, she reached her decision and bypassed him. Luc was exceptionally newsworthy and she could not afford to be seen with him, lest her past catch up with the present that Harriet had so carefully reconstructed for her.

A security man materialised at her elbow and opened the door of the limousine. Ducking her head, she slid along the cream leather upholstery to the far corner. The door slammed on them, sealing them into claustrophobic privacy.

'Really, Catherine . . . was that so difficult?' Luc murmured silkily. 'Would you like a drink?'

Her throat was parched. She fought for her vanished poise. 'Why not?'

Her palms smoothed nervously down over her skirt, rearranging the folds. Her skin prickled at his proximity as he bent forward to press open the built-in bar. For the longest moment of her existence, the black springy depths of his hair were within reach of her fingers. The mingled aroma of some elusive lotion and that indefinable but oh, so familiar scent that was purely him assailed her defensively flared nostrils. As he straightened again, she was disturbingly conscious of the clean movement of rippling muscles beneath the expensive fabric that sheathed his broad shoulders. And an ache and an agony were reborn treacherously within her.

Her hands laced tightly together. In the unrelenting silence, she believed she could hear her own heartbeat, speeding and pounding out the evidence of her own betrayal. She was horrified by the sensual imagery that had briefly driven every other thought from her mind. If her memory was playing tricks on her, her body was no less eager to follow suit.

Luc extended her glass, retaining hold of it long enough to force her to look at him. It was a power-play, a very minor one on Luc's terms but it made her feel controlled. She took several fast swallows of her drink. It hurt her tight throat and she hated the taste, but once she had been naïve enough to drink something she detested because she believed that was sophistication.

'Feel better now?' Luc enquired lazily, lounging back with his brandy in an intrinsically graceful movement. 'Do you live in London?'

'No,' she said hurriedly. 'I'm only here for the day. I live in . . . in Peterborough.'

'And you're married. That must be a source of great satisfaction to you.'

The ring on her wedding finger began to feel like a rope tightening round her vocal chords. She decided to overlook the sarcasm.

'When did you get married?'

'About four years ago.' She took another slug of her drink to fortify herself for the next round of whoppers.

'Shortly after——'

Her brain had already registered her error. 'It was a whirlwind romance,' she proffered in a rush.

'It must have been,' he drawled. 'Tell me about him.'

'It's all very pedestrian,' she muttered. 'I'm sure you can't really be interested.'

'On the contrary,' Luc contradicted softly. 'I am fascinated. Does your husband have a name?'

'Luc, I——'

'So, you remember mine? An unsought compliment...'

She stared down into her glass. 'Paul. He's called Paul.' Fighting the rigid tension threatening her, she managed a small laugh. 'Honestly, you can't want to hear all this!'

'Indulge me,' Luc advised. 'Are you happy living in...where was it? Peterhaven?'

'Yes, of course I am.'

'You don't look very happy.'

'It doesn't always show,' she retorted in desperation.

'Children?' he prompted casually.

Catherine froze, icicles sliding down her spine, and she could not prevent a sudden, darting, upward glance. 'No, not yet.'

Luc was very still. Even in the grip of her own turmoil, she noticed that. And then without warning he smiled. 'What were you doing with Huntingdon?'

The question thrown at her out of context shook her. 'I...I ran into him while I was shopping,' she hesitated and, with a stroke of what seemed to her absolute brilliance, added, 'My husband works for him.'

'You do seem to have enjoyed a day excessively full of coincidences.' Stunning golden eyes whipped over her flushed, heart-shaped face. 'The unexpected is invariably the most entertaining, isn't it?'

She set down her glass. 'I r... really have to be going. It's been... lovely meeting you again.'

'I'm flattered you should think so,' Luc murmured expressionlessly. 'What are you afraid of?'

'Afraid of?' she echoed unsteadily. 'I'm not afraid of anything!' She took a deep, shuddering breath. 'We have nothing to talk about.'

'I foresee a long day ahead of us,' Luc commented.

Catherine bent her head. 'I don't have to answer your questions,' she said tightly, struggling to keep a dismaying tremor out of her voice. Fight fire with fire. That was the only stance to take with Luc.

'Think of it as a small and somewhat belated piece of civility,' Luc advised. 'Four and a half years ago, you vanished into thin air. Without a word, a letter or a hint of explanation. I would like that explanation now.'

Stains of pink had burnished her cheeks. 'In a nutshell, getting involved with you was the stupidest thing I ever did,' she condemned.

'And telling me that may well prove to be your second.' Dark hooded eyes rested on her. 'You slept with me the night before you disappeared. You lay in my arms and you made love with me, knowing that you planned to leave...'

'H-habit,' she stammered.

Hard fingers bit into her wrist, trailing her closer without her volition. 'Habit?' he ground out roughly, incredulously.

Her tongue was glued to the dry roof of her mouth. Mutely she nodded, and recoiled from the raw fury and revulsion she read in his unusually expressive eyes. 'You're hurting me,' she mumbled.

He dropped her wrist contemptuously. 'My compliments, then, on an award-winning performance. Habit inspired you with extraordinary enthusiasm.'

She reddened to the roots of her hair, attacked by the sort of memories she never let out of her subconscious even on temporary parole. To remember was to hate herself. And that night she had known in her heart of hearts that she would never be with Luc again. With uncharacteristic daring, she had woken him up around dawn, charged with a passionate despair that could only find a vent in physical expression. Loving someone who did not love you was the cruellest kind of suffering.

'I don't remember,' she lied weakly, loathing him so much that she hurt with the force of her suppressed emotions. He made her a stranger to herself. He had done that in the past and he was doing it now. She was not the Catherine who understood and forgave other people's foibles at this moment. She had paid too high a price for loving Luc.

'Habit.' He said it again, but so softly; yet she was chilled.

Quite by accident, she registered, she had stung his ego, stirring the primitive depths of a masculinity that was rarely, if ever, challenged by her sex. She wasn't the only woman to make a fool of herself over Luc. Women went to the most embarrassing lengths to attract his attention. They went to even greater lengths to hold him. The reflection was of cold comfort to her.

Women were leisure-time toys for Luc Santini. Easily lifted, just as easily cast aside and dismissed. On the rise to the top, Luc had never allowed himself to waste an ounce of his single-minded energy on a woman. Women had their place in his life...of course they did. He was a very highly sexed male animal. But a woman never held the foreground in his mind, never came between him and his cold, analytical intelligence.

'I have to be going,' she said again and yet, when she collided with that gleaming gaze, she was strangely reluctant to move.

'As you wish.' With disorientating cool, he watched her gather up her bag and climb out of the car on rubbery legs, teetering dangerously for an instant on the very high heels she always wore.

Dragging wayward eyes from his dark, virile features, she closed the door and crossed the street. She felt dizzy, shell-shocked. All those lies, she thought guiltily; all those lies to protect Daniel. Not that Luc could be a threat to Daniel now, but she felt safer with Luc in ignorance. Luc didn't like complications or potential embarrassments. An illegitimate son would qualify as both.

A little dazedly, she shook her head. Apart from that one moment of danger, Luc had been so...so cool. She couldn't say what she had expected, only somehow it hadn't been that. In the Savoy, she could have sworn that Luc was blazingly angry. Obviously that had been her imagination. After all, why should he be angry? Four years was a long time, she reminded herself. And he hadn't cared about her. You didn't constantly remind someone you cared about that they were living on borrowed time. At least, not in Catherine's opinion you didn't.

Her mind drifted helplessly back to their first meeting. She had rewarded his mere presence at the gallery with a guided tour *par excellence*. She had never been that close to a male that gorgeous, that sophisticated and that exciting. Luc, bored with his own company and in no mood to entertain a woman, had consented to be entertained.

He had smiled at her and her wits had gone a-begging, making her forget what she was saying. It hadn't meant anything to him. He had left without even advancing his name but, before he had gone, he said, 'You shouldn't be up here on your own. You shouldn't be so friendly with strangers either. A lot of men would take that as a come-on and you really wouldn't know how to handle that.'

As he'd started down the stairs, glittering golden eyes had glided over her one last time. What had he seen? A pretty, rounded teenager as awkward and as easily read as a child in her hurt disappointment.

In those days, though, she had been a sunny optimist. If he had happened in once, he might happen in again. However, it had been two months before Luc re-appeared. He had walked in late on and alone, just as he had before. Scarcely speaking, he had strolled round the new pictures with patent uninterest while she'd chattered with all the impulsive friendliness he had censured on his earlier visit. Three-quarters of the way back to the exit, he had swung round abruptly and looked back at her.

'I'll wait for you to close up. I feel like some company,' he had drawled.

The longed-for invitation had been careless and last-minute, and the assumption of her acceptance one of unapologetic arrogance. Had she cared? Had she heck!

'I've been shut in all day. I'd enjoy a walk,' he had murmured when she'd pelted breathlessly back to his side.

'I don't mind,' she had said. He could have suggested a winter dip in the Thames and she would have shown willing. Taking her coat from her, he had deftly assisted her into it, and she had been impressed to death by his instinctive good manners.

As first dates went, it had been...different. He had walked her off her feet and treated her to a coffee in an all-night café in Piccadilly. She hadn't had a clue who he was and he had enjoyed that. He had told her about growing up in New York, about his family, the father, mother and sister who had died in a plane crash the previous year. In return she had opened her heart about her own background, contriving to joke as she invariably did about her unknown ancestry.

'Maybe I'll call you.' He had tucked her, alone and unkissed, into a cab to go home.

He hadn't called. Six, nearly seven agonising weeks had crawled past. Her misery had been overpowering. Only when she had abandoned all hope had Luc shown up again. Without advance warning. She had wept all over him with relief and he had kissed her to stop her crying.

He could have turned out to be a gangster after that kiss...it wouldn't have mattered; it wouldn't have made the slightest difference to her feelings. She was in love, hopelessly, crazily in love, and somewhere in the back of her mind she had dizzily assumed that he had to be too. How romantic, she had thought, when he presented her with a single white rose. Later she had bought a flower press to conserve that perfect bloom for posterity...

What utterly repellent things memories could be! Luc didn't have a romantic bone in his body. He had simply set about acquiring the perfect mistress with the same cool, tactical manoeuvres he employed in business. Step one, keep her off balance. Step two, convince her she can't live without you. Step three, move in for the kill. She had been seduced with so much style and expertise that she hadn't realised what was happening to her.

Pick an ordinary girl and run rings round her. That was what Luc had done to her. She might as well have tied herself to the tracks in front of an express train. Every card had been stacked against her from the start.

Glancing at her watch in a crowded street, she was stunned to realise how late it was. Lost in her thoughts she had wandered aimlessly through the afternoon. Without further ado, she headed for the bus-stop.

Drew's housekeeper, Mrs Bugle, was putting on her coat to go home when Catherine let herself into the apartment. 'I'm afraid I was too busy to leave dinner prepared for you, Mrs Parrish,' she said stiffly.

'Oh, that's fine. I'm used to looking after myself.' But Catherine was taken aback by the formerly friendly woman's cold, disapproving stare.

'I want you to know that Mrs Huntingdon is taking this divorce very hard,' Mrs Bugle told her accusingly. 'And I'll be looking for another position if Mr Huntingdon remarries.'

The penny dropped too late for Catherine to speak up in her own defence. With that parting shot, Mrs Bugle slammed the front door in her wake. A prey to a weary mix of anger, embarrassment and frustration, Catherine reflected that the housekeeper's attack was the finishing touch to a truly ghastly day.

So now she was a marriage-wrecker, was she? The other woman. Mrs Bugle would not be the last to make that assumption. Annette Huntingdon's affair was a well-kept secret, known to precious few. Dear God, how could she have been so blind to Drew's feelings?

Harriet had been very much against her brother's desire for a divorce. She had lectured Drew rather tactlessly, making him more angry and defensive than ever at a time when he was already hurt and humiliated by his wife's betrayal.

Had she herself been too sympathetic in an effort to balance Harriet's well-meant insensitivity? When Drew chose to talk to her instead, had she listened rather too well? She had felt desperately sorry for him but she hadn't really wanted to be involved in his marital problems. All she had done was listen, for goodness' sake... and evidently Drew had read that as encouragement.

What she ought to be doing now was walking right back out of this apartment again! But how could she? After paying Mrs Anstey a month's rent in advance, she had less than thirty pounds to her name. Peggy had raged at her frequently for not demanding some sort of a wage for looking after Harriet, whose housekeeper had retired shortly after Catherine had moved in. However, Harriet, always ready to give her last penny away to someone more needy than herself and, let's face it, Catherine acknowledged guiltily, increasingly silly with what little money she did have, could not have afforded to pay her a salary.

And it hadn't mattered, it really hadn't mattered until Harriet had died. With neither accommodation nor food to worry about, Catherine had contrived to make ends meet in a variety of ways. She had registered as a child-minder, although, between Harriet's demands and Daniel's, that had provided only an intermittent income for occasional extras. She had grown vegetables, done sewing alterations, boarded pets... somehow they had always managed. But the uncertainties of their future now loomed over her like a giant black cloud.

As she unpacked, she faced the fact that she would have to apply to the Social Services for assistance until she got on her feet again. And when Drew returned from Germany, she decided, she would tell him about her past. If what he felt for her was the infatuation she suspected it was, he would quickly recover. Either way, she would lose a friendship she had come to value. When she fell off her pedestal with a resounding crash, Drew would feel, quite understandably, that he had been deceived.

The doorbell went at half-past six. She was tempted to ignore it, lest it be someone else eager to misinterpret her presence in the apartment. Unfortunately, whoever was pressing the bell was persistent, and her nerves wouldn't sit through a third shrill burst.

It was Luc. For a count of ten nail-biting seconds, she believed she was hallucinating. As she fell back, her hand slid weakly from the door. 'Luc...?' she whispered.

'I see you haven't made it back to Peterborough yet. Or was it Peterhaven?' Magnificent golden eyes clashed with startled blue. 'You didn't seem too sure where you lived. And you're a lousy liar, *cara*. In fact, you're so poor a liar, I marvel that you even attempted to deceive me. Yet you sat in that car and you lied and lied and lied...'

'Did I?' she gasped, in no state to put her brain into more agile gear.

'Do you know why I let you go this afternoon?' He sent the door crashing shut with one impatient thrust of his hand.

'N-no.'

'If you had told me one more lie in the mood I was in, I would have strangled you,' Luc spelt out. 'Where do you get the courage to lie to me?'

It was nowhere in evidence now. Helplessly she stared at him. He was so very tall and, in the confines of a hall barely big enough to swing the proverbial cat in, he was overpowering. He had all the dark splendour of a Renaissance prince in his arrogant bearing. And he was just as lethally dangerous. As he slid a sun-bronzed hand into the pocket of his well-cut trousers, pulling the fabric taut across lean, hard thighs, she shut her eyes tight on the vibrantly sensual lure of him.

But her mouth ran dry and her stomach clenched in spite of the precaution. Had she really expected to be quite indifferent? To feel nothing whatsoever for this man she had once loved, whose child she had once borne in fearful isolation? Now she knew why she had fled his car in such a state, both defying and denying the existence of responses she had fondly believed she had outgrown with maturity.

A woman met a male of Luc Santini's calibre only once in a lifetime if she was lucky. And forever after, whether she liked it or not, he would be the standard by which she judged other men. She was suddenly frighteningly aware that, in all the years since she had walked out of that Manhattan apartment, no other man had stirred her physically. It had been no sacrifice to ignore the sensuality which had in the past so badly betrayed her. Now she was recognising that facing Luc again had to be the ultimate challenge.

The silence went on and on and on.

'Cristo, cara!' The intervention was disturbingly low-pitched. 'What is it that you think of? You look as though you're about to fall down on your knees and pray for deliverance...'

Her lashes flew up. 'Do I?' It was called playing for time by playing dumb. What was he doing here? What did he want from her? Which lies had he identified as lies? Dear God, did he suspect that she had a child? How could he suspect? she asked herself. Even so, she turned white at the very thought of that threat.

Without troubling to reply, he strode past her to push open the kitchen door and glance in. In complete bewilderment, she watched him repeat the action with each of the remaining doors, executing what appeared to be an ordered search of the premises. What was he looking for? Potential witnesses? Her mythical husband? Or a child? Her flesh grew clammy with fear. In the economic market, Luc was famed for his uncanny omniscience. He noticed what other people didn't notice. He could interpret what was hidden. If he had ever taken the time to focus that powerful intelligence on her disap-

pearance, he would have grasped within minutes that
there was a strong possibility that she was pregnant.

'Did you enjoy yourself trailing my security men all
over town for three hours this afternoon?' Luc enquired
dulcetly, springing her from her increasingly panic-
stricken ruminations.

'Trailing your...?' As she registered his meaning, her
incredulity spoke for her.

'Zero for observation, *cara*. You don't change. You
wander around in a rosy dream-state like an accident
waiting to happen.' He strolled fluidly into the lounge,
his wide mouth compressing as he took open stock of
his surroundings. 'No verdant greenery, not a floral
drape or a frill or a flounce anywhere in sight. Either
you haven't lived here very long or he has imposed his
taste on yours. *Dio*, he had more success than I...'

The last was an aside, as disorientating as the speech
which had preceded it. Unwittingly, she went pink as she
recalled scathing comments about her preference for
nostalgia as opposed to the abrasively modern décors he
favoured. It was an unfortunate reference, summoning
up, as it inexplicably did, stray and rebellious memories
of baths by candlelight and an over-the-top lace-strewn
four-poster bed...

The vast differences between them even on that level
were almost laughable. Two more radically differing
personalities would have been hard to find. Her dreams
had been the ordinary ones of love and marriage and
children.

But Luc hadn't had dreams. Dreams weren't realistic
enough to engage his attention. He lived his life by a
master plan of self-aggrandisement. He achieved one
goal and moved on to the next. The possibility of failure
never occurred to him. It was, after all, unthinkable that
Luc would ever settle for less than what he wanted. As
she thought unavoidably of how much less than her

dreams she had settled for, bitterness coalesced into a hard, unforgiving stone inside her.

'Feel free to make yourself at home.' Her sarcasm was so out of character that Luc whipped round in surprise to stare at her.

'Don't talk to me like that,' he breathed almost tautly.

'I'll talk to you whatever way I want!' she dared.

'Be my guest,' Luc invited. 'You won't do it more than once.'

'Want to bet?' Her ability to defy him was gathering steam on the awareness that neither Daniel nor any trace of him could betray her in this apartment.

'If I were you, I wouldn't risk it,' Luc responded. 'You have this appalling habit of backing the wrong horse. And the odds definitely aren't in your favour.'

Courageously, she lifted her chin. 'I am not afraid of you.'

'You ought to be.'

Her Joan of Arc backbone suffered a sudden jolt in confidence. 'Are you trying to threaten me?' she asked shakily.

'To my knowledge, I've never *tried* to threaten anyone.' It was an assertion backed by immovable cool.

She bent her head. 'I've got nothing to say to you.'

'But I have plenty to say to you.'

'I don't want to hear it.' Jerkily she crossed her arms to conceal the fact that her hands were shaking, and moved over to the window, her back protectively turned on him.

'When I talk to people, I prefer them to look at me,' Luc imparted with irony.

'I don't want to look at you.' She was dismayed to realise that she was perilously close to tears. If wishes were horses, she would have been a thousand miles from this confrontation.

'Since I arrived, I've been having a marvellous conversation with myself.' The sardonic criticism of her monosyllabic responses drove much-needed colour into her cheeks. 'Perhaps I should approach this from a different angle.'

Taking a deep breath, she spun back to him. 'I want you to leave.'

An ebony brow elevated. 'The carpet or me?'

She flung her head back, sharp strain etched into every delicate line of her features, but she said nothing, could not trust her voice to emerge levelly or her gaze to meet directly with his.

'May we dispense with the imaginary husband, whose name you have such difficulty in recalling?' Luc murmured very quietly. 'I don't believe he exists.'

'I don't know where you get that idea.' Wildly disconcerted by the question thrown at her without warning, she was dismally conscious that her reply lacked sufficient surprise or annoyance to be convincing.

'I won't play these games with you.' The victim of that hooded dark stare holding her by sheer force of will, she felt cornered. 'I play them everywhere else in my life, but not with you. I saw you with Huntingdon outside the hotel. No doubt you believe that that ring lends a certain spurious respectability to your present position in his life. It doesn't,' he concluded flatly.

Desperation was beginning to grip her. 'You misunderstood what you saw.'

'Did I? I don't think so,' Luc murmured. 'Relax, he's still all in one piece... but he's halfway to Germany in pursuit of a contract he's not going to get.'

Her lower lip parted company with the upper. 'I b-beg your pardon?'

'You are not, I believe, hard of hearing.'

Unbearable tension held her unnaturally still. 'What have you got to do with that contract?'

'Influence alone,' Luc delivered. 'And influence will be sufficient.'

'But why? I mean, Drew?' she whispered strickenly.

'Unfortunately for him, this is his apartment.' Luc sent her a glittering glance, redolent of unashamed threat. 'And when a man trespasses on my territory, it must hurt. If it does not, who will respect the boundaries I set? Surely you do not expect me to reward him for bedding my woman?'

CHAPTER THREE

CATHERINE went white. Luc was hitting her with too much all at once. It was as if she were drowning and unable to breathe. Shock was reverberating with paralysing effect all the way down from her brain to her toes.

Luc surveyed her without a tinge of remorse. And this time she could sense the savage anger he was containing. A dark aura that radiated violent vibrations into the thickening atmosphere. It was an insidiously intimidating force, for Luc had never lost his temper with her before. Luc rarely unleashed his emotions. People who let anger triumph invariably surrendered control of the situation. Luc would not be guilty of such a gross miscalculation. Or so she had once believed...

She tried and failed to swallow. The tip of her tongue nervously crept out to moisten her dry lips. 'I am not your woman,' she said unsteadily.

Black spiky lashes partially screened a blaze of gold. 'For two years you were mine, indisputably mine, as no other woman ever has been. Some things don't change. In the Savoy, you couldn't take your eyes off me.'

Catherine was so appalled by the accusation that she momentarily forgot the threat to Drew. 'That's nonsense!'

'Is it?' She was reminded of a well-fed tiger indulgently watching his next meal at play. His brilliant gaze was riveted to her. 'I don't believe it is. And why should we argue about it? You have the same effect on me. I'm not denying it. A certain *je ne sais quoi*, unsought and, on many occasions since, unwelcome, but still in existence after six and a half years. Doesn't that tell you something?'

A furrow between her brows, Catherine was struggling to follow what he was telling her, but every time she came close to comprehension she retreated from it in disbelief.

'Plenty of marriages don't last that long,' Luc pointed out smoothly. 'I want you back, Catherine.'

In the bottomless pit of the silence he allowed to fall, she was sure she could hear her own heartbeat thundering fit to burst behind her breastbone. Her throat worked convulsively but no sound emerged, and that was hardly surprising when he had deprived her of the power of speech. Shock had gone into counter-shock, and her capacity to think straight had gone into cold storage.

'You have to be the most incredibly modest woman of my acquaintance. Do you really think I would go to these lengths for anything less?' Strolling over to the table, Luc uncapped one of the decanters, lifted a glass off the tray and poured a single measure of brandy.

'I can't believe that you can say that to me,' she mumbled.

'Console yourself with the reflection that I have not said one quarter of what I would like to say.' Luc slotted the glass between her nerveless fingers, cupped them helpfully round to clasp it, the easy intimacy of his touch one more violently disorientating factor to plague her. 'I feel sure that you are grateful for my restraint.'

Dimly she understood how a rabbit felt, mesmerised by headlights on the motorway. Those golden eyes could be shockingly compelling. The brandy went down in one appreciative gulp and she gasped as fire raced down her throat. It banished her paralysis, however, and retrieved her wits. 'You . . . you actually think that Drew is keeping me?' she demanded with a shudder of distaste. 'Is that what you're insinuating?'

'I rarely insinuate, *cara*. I state.'

'How dare you?' Catherine exclaimed.

Luc dealt her an impassive look. 'I find it particularly unsavoury that he should be a married man, old enough to be your father.'

Restraint, she acknowledged, was definitely fighting a losing battle. Fierce condemnation accompanied that final statement. 'There's nothing unsavoury about Drew!' she protested furiously. 'He's one of the most decent, honourable men I've ever met!'

'Only not above cheating on his wife with a woman half his age,' Luc drawled in biting conclusion. 'A little word of warning, *cara*. After tonight, I don't ever wish to hear his name on your lips again.'

Catherine was too caught up in an outraged defence of Drew to listen to him. 'He wouldn't cheat on his wife. He's been separated from her for almost a year. He'll be divorced next month!'

'I know,' Luc interposed softly, taking the wind from her sails. 'He should have stayed home with his wife. It would have been safer for him.'

'Safer?' she whispered, recalling what he had said some minutes earlier. 'You threatened him——'

'No. I delivered a twenty-two-carat-gold promise of intent.' The contradiction was precise, chilling.

'But you didn't mean it, you couldn't have meant it!' she argued in instinctive appeal.

Dark eyes lingered on her reflectively and veiled. 'If you say so.' A broad shoulder lifted in a very Latin shrug of dismissal. 'We have more important things to discuss.'

Her stomach executed a sick somersault. Under that exquisitely tailored suit dwelt a predator of Neanderthal proportions, ungiven to anything as remote as an attack of conscience. 'It's absolutely none of your business,' she conceded tightly, 'but I'm not having an affair with Drew.'

'Everything that concerns you is my business.'

It went against the grain to permit that to go past unchallenged, but she was more concerned about Drew. 'Why should you want to damage Huntingdon Components? What has he ever done to you?'

'You ask me that?' It was a positive snarl of incredulity. 'You live in his apartment and you ask me that?'

'It's not what it seems.'

'It is exactly what it seems. Cheap, nasty.' His nostrils flared as he passed judgement.

'Like what I had with you?' She couldn't resist the comparison.

'Cristo!' He threw up both hands in sudden lancing fury. 'How can you say that to me? In all my life, I never treated a woman as well as I treated you!'

The most maddening quality of that assurance was its blazing, blatant sincerity. He actually believed what he was saying. Her teeth ground together on a blistering retort.

'And what did I receive in return? You tell me!' he slashed at her rawly, rage masking his dark features. 'A bloody stupid scrawl on a mirror that I couldn't even read! I trusted you as though you were my family and you betrayed that trust. You stuck a knife in my back.'

She should have been better prepared for that explosion, but she wasn't. His legendary self-control had evaporated right before her stricken eyes, revealing the primitive depth of the anger she had dared to provoke. 'Luc, I——'

'Stay where you are!' The command cracked like a whiplash across the room, halting her retreat in the direction of the door. 'You were with me two years, Catherine. Two years,' he repeated fiercely, anger vibrating from every tensed line of his lean, powerful physique. 'And then you vanish into thin air. In nearly five years, what do I get? Hmm? Not so much as a postcard! So, I look for you. I wonder if you're starving somewhere. I worry about how you're managing to live. I think maybe you've had an accident, maybe you're dead. And where do I find you?' he grated in soaring crescendo. 'In the Savoy with another man!'

Her feet were frozen to the carpet under that searing onslaught. She had never seen Luc betray that much emotion. Dazedly, she watched him swing away from her, ferocious tension etched into the set of his broad shoulders and the angle of his hard, taut profile. She could not quite credit the evidence of what she was seeing, never mind what he had said.

He had worried about her? He had actually worried about her? In her mind she fought to come to terms with that revelation. When she had left him, sneaking cravenly out of the service entrance like a thief, she had foreseen his probable response to her departure. Disbelief...outrage...contempt...acceptance. The idea of his worrying about her, looking for her, had never once occurred to her.

In a strange way which she could not understand, she found the idea very disturbing, and it was in reaction to that that she chose to say nothing in her own defence. One fact had penetrated. Luc had no suspicion of Daniel's existence. That fear assuaged, she could only think of Drew.

'Leave Drew alone,' she said. 'He needs that contract.'

'Is that all you have to say to me?' There was a formidable chill in his dark eyes.

She swallowed hard. 'Losing that contract could ruin him.'

A grim smile curved his lips. 'I know.'

'If you're angry with me, take it out on me. I can't believe you really want to harm Drew,' she confided.

'Believe it,' Luc urged.

'I mean...' she made a helpless movement of her small hands, eloquent of her confusion '...you walk in here and you say... you say you want me back, but there's absolutely no question of that,' she completed shakily.

'No?'

'No! And I don't understand why you're doing this to me!' she cried.

'Maybe you should try.'

She refused to look at him. He had hurt her too much. In Luc's presence she was as fearfully wary as a child who had once put her hand in the fire. The memory of the pain was a persistent barrier. 'I won't try,' she said with simple dignity. 'You're an episode which I put behind me a long time ago.'

'An episode?' he derided incredulously. 'You lived with me for two years!'

'Nineteen months, and every month a mistake,' Catherine corrected, abandoning her caution by degrees.

'*Madre de Dio.*' A line of colour demarcated his high cheekbones. 'Hardly a one-night stand.'

Visibly she flinched. 'Oh, I don't know. I often used to feel like one.'

'How can you say that to me? I treated you with respect!' he ground out.

'That was respect?' A chokey laugh escaped her. She felt wild in that instant. If she had been a tigress, she would have clawed him to death in revenge. Her very powerlessness taunted her cruelly. 'When I look at you now, I wonder why it took me so long to come to my senses.'

'Since I arrived, you have looked everywhere but at me,' Luc said drily, deflatingly.

'I hate you, Luc. I hate you so much that if you dropped dead at my feet I'd dance on your corpse!' she vented in a feverish rush.

'The near future promises to be intriguing.'

'There isn't going to be one for us!' Catherine had
never lost her head with anyone before, but it was happening now. As if it were not bad enough that he should
stand there with the air of someone handling an escaped
lunatic with enviable cool, he was ignoring every word
she said. 'I'm not about to fall into line like one of your
employees! Come back to you? You have to be out of
your mind! You used me once, and I'd sooner be dead
than let you do it again! I loved you, Luc. I loved you
much more than you deserved to be loved——'

'I know,' he interposed softly.

A hectic flush carmined her cheeks, fury running
rampant through her every skin-cell. 'What do you
mean...you know? Where do you get the nerve to admit
that?'

Unreadable golden eyes arrowed into her and lingered
intently. 'I thought it might be in my favour.'

'In your favour? It makes what you did to me all the
more unforgivable!' Catherine ranted in a fresh burst of
outrage. 'You took everything I had to give and tried to
pay for it, as though I were some tramp you'd picked
up on a street-corner!'

His jawline clenched. 'I might have made one or two
unfortunate errors of judgement,' he conceded after a
very long pause. 'But, if you were dissatisfied with our
relationship, you should have expressed that
dissatisfaction.'

'I beg your pardon? Expressed it?' Catherine could
hardly get the words out, she was so enraged. 'God
forgive you, Luc, because I never will! Let me just make
one little point. You can go out there and you can buy
anything you want, but you can't buy me. I'm not
available. I'm not up for sale. There's no price-tag at-
tached, so what are you going to do?'

Trembling violently, she turned away from him, emotion still storming through her in a debilitating wave. She had never dreamt that she could attack Luc like that, but somehow it had simply happened. Yet in the aftermath she experienced no sense of pleasure; she felt only pain. A tearing, desperate pain that seemed to encompass her entire being. Just being in the same room with him hurt. She had sworn once that she would not let him do this to her. She would not let hatred poison the very air she breathed. But that wall inside her head was tumbling down brick by brick, and the vengeful force of all the feelings she had buried behind it was surging out of control. With those feelings came memories she fiercely sought to blank out...

That day he had given her the rose, he had escorted her down to a limousine. Cinderella had never had it so good. There had been no glass slipper to fall off at midnight. He had swept her off her feet into a world she had only read about in magazines. He had revelled in her wide eyes, her innocence, her inability to conceal her joy in merely being with him. For five days, she had been lost in a breathless round of excitement. Fancy night-clubs where they danced the night away, intimate meals in dimly lit restaurants... and his last evening in London, of course, in his hotel suite.

But even then Luc hadn't been predictable. When he had reduced her to the clinging, mindless state in his arms after dinner, he had set her back from him with a pronounced attitude of pious self-denial. 'I'm spending Christmas in Switzerland. Come with me,' he had urged lazily as though he were inviting her to merely cross the road.

She had been staggered, embarrassed, uncertain, but she had always been hopelessly sentimental about the festive season. Initially she had said no, uneasy about the prospect of letting Luc pay her way abroad.

'I don't know when I'll be back in London again.' A lie, though she hadn't known it then, as carefully processed as she had been by the preparation of two-month absences between meetings. What Luc didn't know about giving a woman withdrawal symptoms hadn't yet been written.

Convinced that she might lose him forever by letting old-fashioned principles come between them, she had caved in. She had been so dumb that she had expected them to be staying in a hotel in separate rooms. Even in the grip of the belief that she would walk off the edge of the world if he asked her to, she hadn't felt that she had known him long enough for anything else. He had returned to New York. Elaine Gould had been stunned to see a photo of her with Luc in a newspaper the next day. Elaine had tried to reason with her in a curt, well-meaning way. Even her landlady, breathlessly hung on the latest instalment of her romance, had given the thumbs-down to Switzerland. But she had been beyond the reach of sensible advice.

Six hours in an isolated Alpine chalet had been enough to separate her from a lifetime of principles. No seduction had ever been carried out more smoothly. No bride could have been brought to the marital bed with greater skill and consideration than Luc had employed. And, once Luc had taken her virginity, he had possessed her body and soul. She hadn't faced the fact that she knew about as much about having an affair as Luc knew about having a conscience. The towering passion had been there, the man of her dreams had been there, but the wedding had been nowhere on the horizon. She had given up everything for love...oh, you foolish, reckless woman, where were your wits?

'Catherine.' As she sank back to the present, she shivered. That accent still did something precarious to her knees.

'What were you thinking about?'

Blinking rapidly against the sting of tears, she breathed unsteadily, 'You don't want to know.'

'If you come back to me,' Luc murmured expressionlessly, 'I'll let Huntingdon have the contract.'

'Dear God, you can't bargain with a man's livelihood!' she gasped in horror.

'I can and I will.'

'I hate you! I'd be violently ill if you laid a finger on me!' she swore. Her legs were wobbling and she couldn't drag her eyes from his dark, unyielding features.

Unexpectedly, a smile curved his sensual mouth. 'I'll believe that when it happens.'

'Luc, please.' When it came down to it, she wasn't too proud to beg. She could not stand back and allow Drew to suffer by association with her. She could not disclaim responsibility and still live with herself. Luc did not utter idle threats. 'Please think of what you're doing. This is an ego-trip for you...'

A dark brow quirked. 'I've seldom enjoyed a less ego-boosting experience.'

'I can't come back to you, Luc...I just can't. Please go away and forget you ever saw me.' The wobble in her legs had spread dismayingly to her voice.

He drew closer. 'If I could forget you, I wouldn't be here, *cara*.'

Catherine took a hasty step backward. 'Don't you remember all those things I used to do that annoyed you?' she exclaimed in desperation.

'They became endearing when I was deprived of them.'

'Stay away from me!' Hysteria was creeping up on her by speedy degrees as he advanced. 'I'll die if you touch me!'

'And I'll die if I don't. I ought to remind you that I'm a survivor,' Luc drawled almost playfully, reaching for her, golden eyes burning over her small figure in a blaze of hunger. 'You won't remember his name by tomorrow.'

She lunged out of his reach and one of her stiletto heels caught in the fringe of the rug, throwing her right off balance. Her feet went out from under her and she fell, her head bouncing painfully off the edge of something hard. As she cried out, darkness folded in like a curtain falling and she knew no more.

'You can see the area I'm referring to here.' The consultant indicated the shading on the X-ray. 'A previous injury that required quite major surgery. At this stage, however, I have no reason to suspect that she's suffering from anything more than concussion, but naturally she should stay in overnight so that we can keep an eye on her.'

'She's taking a hell of a long time to come round properly.'

'She's had a hell of a nasty bump.' Meeting that narrowed, fierce stare, utterly empty of amusement, the older man mentally matched his facetious response to a lead balloon.

The voices didn't make any sense to Catherine, but she recognised Luc's and was instantly soothed by that recognition. A shard of cut-glass pain throbbed horribly at the base of her skull and, as she shifted her head in a pointless attempt to deaden it, she groaned, her eyes opening on bright light.

Luc swam into focus and she smiled. 'You're all fuzzy,' she mumbled.

A grey-haired man appeared at the other side of the bed and tested her co-ordination. Then he asked her what day it was. She shut her eyes again and thought hard. Her brain felt like so much floating cotton wool. Monday, Tuesday, Wednesday... take your pick. She hadn't a clue what day it was. Come to think of it, she didn't even know what she was doing in hospital.

The question was repeated.

'Can't you see that she's in pain?' Luc demanded in biting exasperation. 'Let her rest.'

'Catherine.' It was the doctor's voice, irritatingly persistent, forcing her to lift her heavy eyelids again. 'Do you remember how you sustained your injury?'

'I've already told you that she fell!' Luc intercepted him a second time. 'Is this interrogation really necessary?'

'I fell,' Catherine whispered gratefully, wishing the doctor would go away and stop bothering her. He was annoying Luc.

'How did you fall?' As he came up with a third question, Luc expelled his breath in an audible hiss and simultaneously the sound of a beeper went off. With a thwarted glance at Luc, the consultant said, 'I'm afraid I'll have to complete my examination in the morning. Miss Parrish will be transferred to her room. Perhaps you'd like to go home, Mr Santini?'

'I'll stay.' It was unequivocal.

Catherine angled a sleepy smile over him, happily basking in the concern he was showing for her well-being. Letting her lashes lower again, she felt the bed she was lying on move. Nurses chattered above her head, complaining about what a wet evening it was, and one of them described some dress she had seen in Marks. It was all refreshingly normal, even if it did make Catherine feel as though she were invisible. Without meaning to, she drifted into a doze.

Waking again, she found herself in a dimly lit, very pleasantly furnished room that didn't mesh with her idea of a hospital. Luc was standing staring out of the window at darkness.

'Luc?' she whispered.

He wheeled round abruptly.

'This may seem an awfully stupid question,' she muttered hesitantly. 'But where am I?'

'This is a private clinic.' He approached the bed. 'How do you feel?'

'As though someone slugged me with a sandbag, but it's not nearly as bad as it was.' She moved her head experimentally on the pillow and winced.

'Lie still,' Luc instructed unnecessarily.

She frowned. 'I don't remember falling,' she acknowledged in a dazed undertone. 'Not at all.'

Luc moved closer, looking less sartorially splendid than was his wont. His black hair was tousled, his tie crumpled, the top two buttons of his silk shirt undone at his brown throat. 'It was my fault,' he said tautly.

'I'm sure it wasn't,' Catherine soothed in some surprise.

'It was.' Dark eyes gleamed down at her almost suspiciously. 'If I hadn't tried to pull you into my arms when you were trying to get away from me, it wouldn't have happened.'

'I was trying to get away from you?' Nothing in her memory-banks could come to terms with that startling concept.

'You tripped over a rug and went down. You struck your head on the side of a table. *Madre de Dio, cara* . . . I thought you'd broken your neck!' Luc relived with unfamiliar emotionalism, a tiny muscle pulling tight at the corner of his compressed mouth. 'I thought you were dead . . . I really thought you were dead.' The repetition was harsh, not quite steady.

'I'm sorry.' A vaguely panicky sensation was beginning to nudge at her nerve-endings. If Luc hadn't been there, it would have swallowed her up completely. Yet his intent stare, his whole demeanour was somehow far from reassuring. Other little oddities, beyond her inability to recall her fall, were springing to mind. 'The nurses...that doctor...they were English. Are we in England?' she demanded shakily.

'Are *we*——?' He put a strange stress on her choice of pronoun, his strong features shuttered, uncommunicative. 'We're in London. Don't you know that?' he probed very quietly.

'I don't remember coming to London with you!' Catherine admitted in a stricken rush. 'Why don't I remember?'

Luc appraised her for a count of ten seconds before he abandoned his stance at a distance and dropped down gracefully on to the side of the bed. 'You've got concussion and you're feeling confused. That's all,' he murmured calmly. 'Absolutely nothing to worry about.'

'I can't help being worried—it's scary!' she confided.

'You have nothing to be scared of.' Luc had the aspect of someone carefully de-programming a potential hysteric.

Her fingers crept into contact with the hand he had braced on the mattress and feathered across his palm in silent apology. 'How long have we been in London?'

Luc tensed. 'Is that important?' As he caught her invasive fingers between his and carried them to his mouth, it suddenly became a matter of complete irrelevance.

Watching her from beneath a luxuriant fringe of ebony lashes, he ran the tip of his tongue slowly along each individual finger before burying his lips hotly in the centre of her palm. A quiver of weakening pleasure lanced through her and an ache stirred in her pelvis. It was incredibly erotic.

'Is it?' he prompted.

'Is...what?' she mumbled, distanced from all rational thought by the power of sensation.

Disappointingly, he laid her hand back down, but he retained a grip on it, a surprisingly fierce grip. 'What is the last thing you remember?'

With immense effort, she relocated her thinking processes and was rewarded. Remembering the answer to that question was as reassuringly easy as falling off the proverbial log. 'You had the flu,' she announced with satisfaction.

'The flu.' Black brows drew together in a frown and then magically cleared again. '*Si*, the flu. That was nineteen eighty——'

She wrinkled her nose. 'I do know what year it is, Luc.'

'*Senz'altro*. Of course you do. The year improves like a good vintage.' As she looked up at him uncomprehendingly, he bent over her with a faint smile and smoothed a stray strand of wavy hair from her creased forehead.

'It seems so long ago, and, when I think about it, it seems sort of hazy,' she complained.

'Don't think about it,' Luc advised.

'Is it late?' she whispered.

'Almost midnight.'

'You should go back to the hotel . . . are we in a hotel?' she pressed, anxious again.

'Stop worrying. It'll all come back,' Luc forecast softly. 'Sooner or later. And then we will laugh about this, I promise you.'

His thumb was absently stroking her wrist. She raised her free hand, powered by an extraordinarily strong need just to touch him, and traced the stubborn angle of his hard jawline. His dark skin was blue-shadowed, interestingly rough in texture. He had mesmeric eyes, she reflected dizzily, dark in shadow or dissatisfaction, golden in sunlight or passion. Vaguely she wondered why he wasn't kissing her.

In that department, Luc never required either en- couragement or prompting. When he came back from a business trip, he swept through the door, snatched her into his arms and infrequently controlled his desire long enough to reach the bedroom. And when he was with her it sometimes seemed that she couldn't cook or clean or do anything without being intercepted.

It made her feel safe. It made her feel that where there was that much passion, surely there was hope. Only of late she had listened less willingly to another little voice. It was more pessimistic. It told her that expecting even the tiniest commitment from Luc where the future was concerned was comparable with believing in the tooth-fairy.

'I've only forgotten a few weeks, haven't I?' she checked, hastily pushing away those uneasy thoughts which made her so desperately insecure.

'You have forgotten nothing of import.' Brilliant eyes shimmered over her upturned face, meeting hers with the zap of a force-field, and yet still, inconceivably to her, he kept his distance.

'Luc——' she hesitated '—what's wrong?'

'I'm getting very aroused. *Dio*, how can you do this to me just by looking at me?' he breathed with sudden ferocity. 'You're supposed to be sick.'

She didn't know which of them moved first but suddenly he was as close as she wanted him to be and her fingers slid ecstatically into the springy depths of his hair. But, instead of the forceful assault his mood had somehow led her to anticipate, he outlined her parted lips with his tongue and then delved between, tasting her with a sweet, lancing sensuality again and again until her head was spinning and her bones were melting and a hunger more intense than she had ever known leapt and stormed through her veins.

With an earthy groan of satisfaction, Luc dragged her up into his arms and, although the movement jarred her painfully, she was more than willing to oblige him. Thrusting the bedding impatiently away from her, he lifted her and brought her down on his hard thighs without once removing his urgent mouth from hers.

Excitement spiralled as suddenly as summer lightning between them. Wild, hot and primeval. His hand yanked at the high neck of the white hospital gown, loosening it, drawing it away from her upper body. Cooler air washed her exposed skin as he held her back from him, lean hands in a powerful grip on her slender arms. A dark flush over his hard cheekbones, he ran raking golden eyes over the fullness of her pale breasts, the betraying tautness of the pink nipples that adorned them.

Reddening beneath that unashamed, heated appraisal, she muttered feverishly, 'Take me back to the hotel.'

Luc shook her by saying something unrepeatable and closing his eyes. A second later, he wrenched the gown back up over her again, stood up and lowered her into the bed. Tucking the light covers circumspectly round her again, he breathed, '*Chiedo scusa.* I'm sorry. You're not well.'

'I'm fine,' she protested. 'I don't want to stay here.'

'You're staying.' He undid the catch on the window and hauled it up roughly, letting a cold breeze filter into the room. 'You're safer here.'

'Safer?'

'Do you believe in fate, *cara*?'

Her lashes fluttered in bemusement and she turned her head on the pillow. Luc, who had been aghast and then vibrantly amused by her devotion to observing superstitions such as not walking under ladders, avoiding stepping on black lines...Luc was asking her about fate? He looked deadly serious as well. 'Of course I do.'

'One shouldn't fight one's fate,' Luc mused, directing a gleaming smile at her. 'You believe that, don't you?'

She had never had an odder conversation with Luc and she was so exhausted that it was an effort to focus her thoughts. 'I think it would be almost impossible to fight fate.'

'I've no intention of fighting it. It's played right into my hands, after all. Go to sleep, *cara*,' he murmured softly. 'We're flying to Italy in the morning.'

'I-Italy?' she parroted, abruptly shot back into wakefulness.

'Don't you think it's time we regularised our situation?'

Catherine stared at him blankly, one hundred per cent certain that he couldn't mean what she thought he meant.

Luc strolled back to the bed and sank down in the armchair beside her, fixing dark glinting eyes on her. 'I'm asking you to marry me.'

'Are you?' She was so staggered by the assurance that it was the only thing she could think to say.

He scored a reflective fingertip along the line of her tremulous bottom lip. 'Say something?' he invited.

'Have you been thinking of this for long?' she managed jerkily, praying for the shock to recede so that she could behave a little more normally.

'Let's say it crept up on me,' he suggested lightly.

That didn't sound very romantic. Muggers crept up on you; so did old age. A paralysing sense of unreality assailed her. Luc was asking her to marry him. That meant she had been living with a stranger for months. That meant that every disloyal, ungenerous thought she had ever had about him had been wickedly unjustified. Tears welled up in her eyes. Lines of moisture left betraying trails down her pale cheeks.

'What did I say? What didn't I say?' Luc demanded. 'OK, so this is not how you imagined me proposing.'

'I never imagined you proposing!' she sobbed.

With a succinct expletive, he slid his hands beneath her very gently and tugged her on to his lap, hauling off the light bedspread and wrapping it round her. She sniffed and sucked in oxygen, curving instinctively in the heat of him. 'I'm so h-happy,' she told him.

'You have a very individual way of being happy, but then,' a caressing hand smoothed through her silky, tumbled hair, 'you have an individual way of doing most things. We'll get married in Italy. And now that we've decided to do it, we don't want to waste time, do we?'

She rested her head against his chest as he lounged back into a more comfortable position to accommodate her. He was being so gentle and once she had honestly believed that he didn't know how to be. Had her fall given him that much of a shock? Certainly something had provoked an astonishing alteration in Luc's attitude to her ... or had she really never understood Luc at all? Did it matter if she couldn't understand him? She decided it didn't.

Luc was planning the wedding. The royal 'we' did not mislead her. She could have listened to him talk all night, but the kind of exhaustion that was a dead weight on her senses was slowly but surely dragging her towards sleep.

CHAPTER FOUR

THE sapphire-blue suit was unfamiliar but it had 'bought to please Luc' stamped in its designer-chic lines. The shoes? Catherine grimaced at the low heels which added little to her diminutive height. She must have been in a tearing hurry when she chose them. They weren't her style at all, but they were a perfect match for the suit. Since co-ordinating her wardrobe had never been one of her talents, she was surprised by the discovery. Luc must have ransacked her luggage to pull off such a feat.

He had been gone when she'd woken, securely back within her bed. Her clothes had arrived after breakfast. Although the effort involved had left her weak, she had been eager to get dressed. A nurse had lightly scolded her for not asking for assistance, adding that Mr Ladwin, the resident consultant, would be in to see her shortly. Catherine couldn't help hoping that Luc arrived first. The prospect of a barrage of probing questions which she wouldn't be able to answer unnerved her.

So, a few weeks had sort of got lost, she told herself bracingly. A few weeks didn't qualify as a real loss of memory, did it? Subduing the panicky sensation threatening, she sat down in the armchair. Of course it would come back and, as Luc had pointed out, it wasn't as though she had forgotten anything important.

Even so, the silliest little things kept on stirring her up. When had she had her hair cut to just below her shoulders? And it was a mess, a real mess! Heaven knew when she had last had a trim. Then there were her hands. She might have been scrubbing floors with them! And there was this funny little dent on her wedding finger, almost as if she had been wearing a ring, and she never put a ring on that finger...

She didn't even recognise the contents of her handbag. She had hoped that something within its capacious depths might jog her memory. She had hoped in vain. Even the purse had been unfamiliar, containing plenty of cash in both dollars and sterling but no credit cards and no photos of Luc. Even the cosmetics she presumably used every day hadn't struck a chord. And where was her passport?

Luc's proposal last night already had a dream-like quality. Luc hadn't been quite Luc as she remembered him. That was the most bewildering aspect of all.

When she had broken an ankle in Switzerland last year, Luc had been furious. He said she was the only person he knew who could contrive to break a limb in the Alps without ever going near a pair of skis. He had stood over her in the casualty unit, uttering biting recriminations about the precarious height of the heels she favoured. The doctor had thought he was a monster of cruelty, but Catherine had known better.

Her pain had disturbed him and he had reacted with native aggression to that disturbance in his usually well-disciplined emotions. Telling her that he'd break her neck if he ever saw her in four-inch stilettos again had been the uncensored equivalent of a major dose of sympathetic concern.

But last night, Luc hadn't been angry...Luc had asked her to marry him. And how could that seem real to her? Her wretched memory had apparently chosen to block out a staggeringly distinct change in her relationship with Luc. Her very presence in London with him when he always jetted about the world alone fully illustrated that change in attitude. But what exactly had brought about that change?

She could not avoid a pained recall of the women Luc had appeared with in newsprint in recent months. Beautiful, pedigreed ladies, who took their place in high society without the slightest doubt of their right to be there. Socialites and heiresses and the daughters of the rich and influential. Those were the sort of women Luc was seen in public with—at charity benefits, movie premières, Presidential dinners.

'I don't sleep with them,' Luc had dismissed her accusations, but still it had hurt. She had looked into the mirror that day and seen her own inadequacy reflected, and she had never felt the same about herself since. It was agonising to be judged and found wanting without ever being aware that there had been a trial.

The door opened abruptly. Luc entered with the consultant in tow. Sunk within the capacious armchair, tears shimmering on her feathery lashes, she looked tiny and forlorn and defenceless in spite of her expensive trappings.

Luc crossed the room in one stride and hunkered down lithely at her feet, one brown hand pushing up her chin. 'Why are you crying?' he demanded. 'Has someone upset you?'

If someone had, they would have been in for a rough passage. Luc was all Italian male in that instant. Protective, possessive, ready to do immediate battle on her behalf. Beneath the cool façade of sophistication, Luc was an aggressively masculine male with very unliberated views on sexual equality. His golden eyes were licking flames on her in over-bright scrutiny. 'If someone has, I want to know about it.'

'I seriously doubt that any of our staff would be guilty of such behaviour.' Mr Ladwin bristled at the very suggestion.

Luc dropped a pristine handkerchief on her lap and vaulted upright. 'Catherine's very sensitive,' he said flatly.

Catherine was also getting very embarrassed. Hastily wiping at her damp cheeks, she said, 'The staff have been wonderful, Luc. I'm just a little weepy, that's all.'

'As I have been trying to explain to you for the past half-hour, Mr Santini,' the consultant murmured, 'amnesia is a distressing condition.'

'And, as you also explained, it lies outside your field.'

Catherine studied the two men uneasily. The undertones were decidedly antagonistic. Ice had dripped from every syllable of Luc's response.

Mr Ladwin looked at her. 'You must feel very confused, Miss Parrish. Wouldn't you prefer to remain here for the present and see a colleague of mine?'

The threat of anything coming between her and the wedding Luc had described so vividly filled Catherine with rampant dismay. 'I want to leave with Luc,' she stressed tautly.

'Are you satisfied?' Luc enquired of the other man.

'It would seem that I have to be.' Scanning the glow that lit Catherine's face when she looked at Luc Santini, the older man found himself wondering with faint envy what it felt like to be loved like that.

Mr Ladwin shook hands and departed. Luc smiled at her. 'The car's outside.'

'I can't find my passport,' she confided abruptly, steeling herself for the disappearance of that smile. Luc got exasperated when she mislaid things.

'Relax,' he urged. 'I have it.'

She sighed relief. 'I thought I'd lost it . . . along with my credit cards and some photos I had.'

'You left them behind in New York.'

She smiled at the simplicity of the explanation. Her usual disorganisation appeared to be at fault.

'Why were you crying?'

She laughed. 'I don't know,' she said, but she did. 'Has someone upset you?' he had demanded with a magnificent disregard for the obvious. Nobody could hurt her more than Luc and, conversely, nobody could make her happier. Loving Luc put her completely in his power and, for the first time in a very long time, she no longer felt she had to be afraid of that knowledge.

A brown forefinger skimmed the vulnerable softness of her lower lip. 'When I'm here, you don't have to worry about anything,' he censured.

Since meeting Luc, worry had become an integral part of her daily existence. The sharp streak of insecurity ingrained in her by her rootless childhood had been roused from dormancy. But it wasn't going to be like that any more, she reminded herself. As Luc's wife, she would hold a very different position in his scheme of what was important. Depressingly, however, when she struggled to picture herself in that starring role, it still felt like fantasy.

'Why do you want to marry me?' Her hands clenched fiercely together as she forced out that bald enquiry in the lift.

'I refuse to imagine my life without you.' He straightened the twisted collar of her silk blouse and tucked the label out of sight with deft fingers. 'Do you think we could save this very private conversation for a less public moment?' he asked lazily.

Catherine made belated eye-contact with the smiling elderly couple sharing the lift with them and reddened to her hairline. She had been too bound up in her own emotions to notice that they had company. Catherine Santini. Secretly she tasted the name, savoured it, and the upswell of joy she experienced was intense.

'Life doesn't begin with "once upon a time", *cara*, and end "and they all lived happily ever after", Luc had once derided. But, regardless, Luc had just presented her with her dream, gift-wrapped and tagged. Evidently if you hoped hard enough and prayed hard enough, it could happen.

As she crossed to the limousine, the heat of the sun took her by surprise. Her eyes scanned the climbing roses in bloom at the wall bounding the clinic's grounds and her stomach lurched violently. 'It's summer,' she whispered. 'You had the flu in September.'

With inexorable cool, Luc pressed her into the waiting car. Her surroundings were then both familiar and re-assuring, but still she trembled. Luc hadn't said a word. Of course, he had known. He had known that she had lost more than a few weeks, had seen no good reason to increase her alarm. Everything now made better sense. No wonder Mr Ladwin had been reluctant to see her leave so quickly. No wonder she didn't recognise her clothes or her hairstyle or the change in Luc. She had lost almost a year of her life.

'Luc, what's happening to me?' she said brokenly. 'What's going on inside my head?'

'Don't try to force it.' His complete calm was won-drously soothing. 'Ladwin advised me not to fill in the blanks for you. He said you should have rest and peace and everything you wanted within reason. Your memory will probably come back naturally, either all at once or in stages.'

'And what if it doesn't?'

'We'll survive. You didn't forget me.' Satisfaction blazed momentarily in his stunning eyes before he veiled them.

The woman who could forget Luc Santini hadn't been born yet. You could love him passionately, hate him passionately, but you couldn't possibly forget him. Hate him? Her brow creased at that peculiar thought and she wondered where it had come from.

'Are you thinking of putting off the wedding?' she asked stiffly. It was the obvious thing to do, the sensible thing to do. And what she most feared was the obvious and the sensible.

'Is that what you want?'

Vehemently she shook her head, refusing to meet his too perceptive gaze. How could she still be so afraid of losing him? He had asked her to marry him. What more could he do? What more could she want?

He didn't love her, he still didn't love her. If she was winning through, it was by default and staying power. She wasn't demanding or difficult, spoilt or imperious. She was loyal and trustworthy and crazy about children. She had had no other lovers. Luc would have a problem coming to terms with a woman who had a past to match his own. And in the bedroom . . . her skin heated at the acknowledgement that she never said no to him, could hardly contain her pleasure when he touched her. Most importantly of all, perhaps, she loved him, and he was content to be loved as long as she never asked for more than he was prepared to give. All in all, he wasn't so much marrying her as promoting her and, though her pride warred against that reality, it was better than severance pay.

'The wedding will take place within a few days,' Luc drawled casually and, picking up the phone, he began the first of several calls. Finding himself the focus of her attention, a smile of almost startling brilliance slashed his hard mouth and he extended a hand, drawing her under the shelter of his arm. 'You look happy,' he said approvingly.

Only a woman who was fathoms deep in love could lose a year of her life and still be happy. Kicking off her shoes, she rested blissfully back into the lean heat of him, thinking she had to be the luckiest woman alive.

Maybe if she worked incredibly hard at being a perfect wife, he might fall in love with her.

'We're in a traffic jam,' she whispered teasingly, tugging at the end of his tie, feeling infinitely more daring than she had ever felt before. The awareness that they would soon be married was dissolving her usual inhibitions.

Luc tensed into sudden rigidity and stumbled over what he was saying. Leaning over him, bracing one hand on a taut thigh, Catherine reached up and loosened his tie, trailing it off in what she hoped was a slow, seductive fashion.

'Catherine . . . what are you doing?'

Luc was being abnormally obtuse. Colliding with golden eyes that had a stunned stillness, she went pink and, lowering her head, embarked on the buttons of his shirt. Hiding a mischievous smile, she understood his incredulity. Undressing Luc was a first. Initiating lovemaking was also a first. She ran caressing fingertips over warm golden skin roughened by black curling hair. His audible intake of oxygen matched to the raw tension in his muscles encouraged her to continue.

There was so much pleasure in simply touching him. It was extraordinary, she thought abstractly, but, although sanity told her it couldn't be possible, she felt starved of him. As she pressed her lips lovingly to his vibrant flesh and kissed a haphazard trail of increasing self-indulgence from his strong brown throat to his flat muscular stomach, he jerked and dropped the phone.

'Catherine . . .' he muttered, sounding satisfyingly ragged.

Her small hand strayed over his thigh. As she touched him he groaned deep in his throat and a sense of wondering power washed over her. He was trembling, his dark head thrown back, a fevered flush accentuating his hard bone-structure. All this time and it was this easy, she reflected, marvelling at the sheer strength of his response to her.

'Catherine, you shouldn't be doing this.' He was breathing fast and audibly, the words thick and indistinct.

'I'm enjoying myself,' she confided, slightly dazed by what she was doing, but telling the truth.

'*Per amor di Dio*, where's my conscience?' he gasped as she ran the tip of her tongue along his waistband.

'What conscience?' she whispered, lost in a voluptuous world all of her own as she inched down his straining zip.

'*Cristo*, this is purgatory!' Taking her by surprise, Luc jackknifed out of reach at accelerated speed. 'We can't do this. We're nearly at the airport!' he muttered unsteadily.

'We're in a traffic jam.' In an agony of mortification more intense than any she had ever known, she stared at him, her hauntingly beautiful eyes dark with pain.

With a succinct swear-word, he dragged her close, taking her mouth with a wild, ravishing hunger that drove the breath from her lungs and left her aching for more. Every nerve-ending in her body went crazy in that powerful embrace. Plastered to every aroused line of his taut length, the scent of him and the taste of him and the feel of him went to her head with the potency of a mind-blowing narcotic.

Dragging his mouth from hers, he buried his face in her tumbled hair. The sharp shock of separation hurt. His heart was crashing against her crushed breasts. She could literally feel him fighting to get himself back under control. A long, shuddering breath ran through him. 'You're not strong enough for this, Catherine. You're supposed to be resting,' he reminded her almost roughly. 'So, have a little pity, hmm? Don't torture me.'

'I'm not ill. I feel great.' She ignored the throbbing at the base of her skull.

With a hard glance of disagreement, he set her back on the seat. 'You're quite capable of saying that because you think that's what I want to hear. How could you feel great? You must feel lousy, and, the next time I ask, lousy is what I want to hear! Is that clear?'

'As crystal.' Bowing her head, she fought to suppress the silent explosion of amusement that had crept up on her unawares. Why was she laughing? Why the heck was she laughing? Her body was shrieking at the deprivation he had sentenced them both to suffer. It wasn't funny, it really wasn't funny, but if she went to her dying day she would cherish the look of disbelief on his dark features when she, and not he, took the initiative for a change.

She had shocked Luc, actually shocked him. Who would ever have dreamt that she could possess that capability? It made her feel wicked... it made her feel sexy... and his reaction had made her feel like the most wildly seductive woman in the world. And wasn't it sweet, incredibly sweet of her supremely self-centred Luc to embrace celibacy for her benefit?

Once, she was convinced, Luc would have taken her invitation at face value, satisfying his own natural inclinations without further thought. That he *had* thought meant a great deal to her. That brand of unselfish caring was halfway to love, wasn't it? In a state of bliss, Catherine listened to him reeling off terse instructions to some unfortunate, no doubt quailing at the other end of the phone line. She wanted to smile. She knew why Luc was in a bad mood.

They traversed the airport at speed in a crush of moving bodies, security men zealously warding off the reporters and photographers Luc deplored. He guarded his privacy with a ferocity that more than one newspaper had lived to regret.

'Who's the blonde, Mr Santini?' someone shouted raucously.

Without warning, Luc wheeled round, his arm banding round Catherine in a hold of steel. 'The future Mrs Santini,' he announced, taking everyone by surprise, including Catherine.

There was a sudden hush and then a frantic clamour of questions, accompanied by the flash of many cameras. Luc's uncharacteristic generosity towards the Press concluded there.

They were crossing the tarmac to the jet when it happened. Something dark and dreadful loomed at the back of her mind and leapt out at her. The sensation frightened the life out of her and she froze. She saw an elderly woman with grey hair, her kindly face distraught. 'You mustn't do it...you mustn't!' she was pleading. And then the image was gone, leaving Catherine white and dizzy and sick with only this nameless, irrational fear focused on the jet.

'I can't get on it!' she gasped.

'Catherine.' Luc glowered down at her.

'I can't...I can't! I don't know why, but I can't!' Hysteria blossoming, she started to back away with raised hands.

Luc strode forward, planted powerful hands to her narrow waist and swung her with daunting strength into his arms. In the grip of that incomprehensible panic, she struggled violently. 'I can't get on that jet!'

'It's not your responsibility any more.' Luc held her with steely tenacity. 'I'm kidnapping you. Think of it as an elopement. Good afternoon, Captain Edgar. Just ignore my fiancée. She's a little phobic about anything that flies without feathers.'

The pilot struggled visibly to keep his facial muscles straight. 'I'll keep it smooth, Mr Santini.'

Luc mounted the steps two at a time, stowed Catherine into a seat and did up the belt much as though it were a ball and chain to keep her under restraint. He gripped her hands. 'Now breathe in slowly and pull yourself together,' he instructed. 'You can scream all the way to Rome if you like but it's not going to get you anywhere. Think of this as the first day of the rest of your life.'

Gasping in air, she stared at him, wide-eyed. 'I saw this woman. I remembered something. She said I mustn't do it...'

'Do what?'

'She didn't say what.' Already overwhelmingly aware of the foolishness of her behaviour, her voice sank to a limp mumble. 'I had this feeling that I shouldn't board the jet, that I was leaving something behind. It was so powerful. I felt so scared.'

'Do you feel scared now?'

'No, of course not.' She flushed. 'I'm sorry. I went crazy, didn't I?'

'You had a flashback. Your memory's returning.'

'Do you think so?' She brightened, was faintly puzzled by his cool tone and the hard glitter of his gaze. 'Why was I so scared?'

'The shock and the suddenness of it,' he proffered smoothly. 'It couldn't have been a comforting experience.'

The flight lasted two hours. They were not alone. There was the steward and the stewardess, the two security men, a sleek executive type taking notes every time Luc spoke, and a svelte female secretary at his elbow, passing out files and removing them and relaying messages. And the weird part of it all was that if Catherine looked near any of them they hurriedly looked away as if she had the plague or something.

Sitting in solitary state, she beckoned the stewardess. 'Could I have a magazine?'

'There are no magazines or newspapers on board, Miss Parrish. I'm so sorry.' The woman's voice was strained, her eyes evasive. 'Would you like lunch now?'

'Thanks.' It was quite peculiar that there shouldn't even be a magazine on board. Still, she would only have flicked through it. Sooner or later, she would have to tell Luc that she was dyslexic. She cringed at the prospect. She had never expected to be able to fool Luc this long. But somehow he had always made it so easy for her.

If there was a menu in the vicinity, he ordered her meals. He accepted that she preferred to remember phone messages rather than write them down for him, and was surprisingly tolerant when she forgot the details. He never mentioned the rarity with which she read a book. Occasionally she bought one and left it on display, but he never asked what it was about. And why did she go to all that trouble?

She remembered how often she had been called stupid before the condition was diagnosed at school. She remembered all the potential foster parents who had backed off at the very mention of dyslexia, falsely assuming that she would be more work and trouble than any other child. She also remembered all the people who had treated her as though she were illiterate. And if Luc realised he was taking on a wife to whom the written word was almost a blur of disconnected images, he might change his mind about marrying her.

When they landed in Rome, he told her that they were completing their journey by helicopter. 'Where will we be staying?' she prompted.

'We won't be staying anywhere,' he countered. 'We're coming home.'

'Home?' she echoed. 'You've bought a house?'

Luc shifted a negligent hand. 'Wait and see.'

'I haven't been there before, have I? It's not something else that I've forgotten, is it?'

'You've never been in Italy before,' he soothed.

She hated the helicopter and insisted on a rear seat, refusing the frontal bird's-eye view that Luc wanted her to have. The racket of the rotors and her sore head interacted unpleasantly, upsetting her stomach. She kept her head down, only raising it when they touched down on solid ground again.

Luc eased her out into the fresh air again, murmuring, 'Lousy?'

'Lousy,' she gulped.

'I should've thought of that, but I wanted you to see Castelleone from the air.' Walking her way from the helipad, he carefully turned her round. 'This is quite a good vantage point. What do you think?'

If he hadn't been supporting her, her knees would have buckled at the sight which greeted her stunned eyes. Castelleone was a fairy-tale castle with a forest of towers and spires set against a backdrop of lush, thickly wooded hills. Late-afternoon sunlight glanced off countless gleaming windows and cast still reflections of the cream stone walls on the water-lily-strewn moat. She should have been better prepared. She should have known to think big and, where Luc was concerned, think extravagant. He might have little time for history but with what else but history could he have attained a home of such magnificence and grandeur?

'It wasn't for sale when I found it, and it wasn't as pretty as it is now...'

'*Pretty?*' she protested, finding her tongue again. 'It's beautiful! It must have cost a fortune.'

'I've got money to burn and nothing else to spend it on.' Idle fingertips slid caressingly through her hair. 'It's a listed building, which is damnably inconvenient. The renovations had to be restorations. Experts are very interfering people. There were times when I wouldn't have cared if those walls came tumbling down into that chocolate-box moat.'

'You're joking!' she gasped.

'Am I? Have you ever lived with seventeenth-century plumbing, *cara*? It was barbaric,' Luc breathed above her head. 'The experts and I came to an agreement. The plumbing went into a museum and I stopped threatening to fill in the moat. We understood each other very well after that.'

'You said it wasn't for sale when you first saw it.'

'For everything there is a price, *bella mia*.' With a soft laugh, he linked his arms round her. 'The last owner had no sentimental attachment to the place. It had been a drain on his finances for too long.'

'Did you ever tell me about it?'

'I wanted to surprise you.' He guided her towards the elaborate stone bridge spanning the moat. Tall studded doors stood wide on a hall covered with exquisitely painted frescoes.

'I've never seen anything so beautiful,' she whispered.

'Admittedly not everyone has a foyer full of fat cherubs and bare-breasted nymphs. I'll concede that if I concede nothing else,' Luc said mockingly. 'The original builder wasn't over-endowed with good taste.'

'If you don't like it, why did you buy it?' she pressed, struggling to hold back her tiredness.

He moved a broad shoulder. 'It's an investment.'

'Does that mean you plan to sell it again?' Her dismay was evident.

'Not if you feel you can live with all those naked women.'

'I can live with them!'

'Somehow,' he murmured softly, 'I thought you would feel like that.'

Luc appraised her pallor, the shadows like bruises below her eyes, and headed her to the curving stone staircase. 'Bed, I think.'

'I don't want to go to bed. I want to see the whole castle.' If it was a dream that Luc should want to marry her and live in this glorious building, she was afraid to sleep lest she wake up.

'You've had all the excitement you can take for one day.' Luc whipped her purposefully off her feet when she showed signs of straying in the direction of an open doorway. 'Why are you smiling like that?'

'Because I feel as though I've died and gone to heaven and——' she hesitated, sending him an adoring look '—I love you so much.'

Dark blood seared his cheekbones, his jawline hardening. Unconcerned, she linked her arms round his throat. 'I'm not a plaster saint,' he breathed.

'I can live with your flaws.'

'You'll have to live with them,' he corrected. 'Divorce won't be one of your options.'

She winced, pained by that response. 'It isn't very romantic to talk about divorce before the wedding.'

'Catherine...as you ought to know by now, I'm not a very romantic guy. I'm not poetic, I'm not sentimental, I'm not idealistic,' he spelt out grimly.

'You make love in Italian,' she said in a small voice.

'It's the first language I ever spoke!'

For some peculiar reason, he was getting angry. She decided to let him have his own way. If he didn't think sweeping her off to a castle in Italy and marrying her within days was romantic, he had a problem. It might be wise, she decided, to share a little less of her rapture. But it was very difficult. Feeling weak and exhausted didn't stop her from wanting to pin him to the nearest horizontal surface and smother him with grateful love and kisses.

At the top of that unending staircase, Luc paused to introduce her to a little man called Bernardo, who rejoiced in the title of major-domo. Catherine beamed at him.

'Do you think you could possibly pin those dizzy feet of yours back to mother earth for a while?' Luc enquired sardonically.

'Not when you're carrying me,' she sighed.

Thrusting open a door, he crossed a large room and settled her down on a bed. It was a four-poster, hung with tassels and fringes and rich brocade. She rested back with a groan of utter contentment, lifted one leg and kicked off a shoe, repeated the action with the other. It was definitely her sort of bed.

His expressive mouth quirked. 'I've arranged for a doctor to see you in half an hour. Do you think you could manage to look less as though you've been at the sherry?'

'What do I need another doctor for?'

A smile angled over her. 'Amnesia is a distressing condition, or so the story goes. I've never seen you like this...at least,' he paused, 'not in a long time.'

'You've never asked me to marry you before,' she whispered shyly.

'A serious oversight. You've never tried to seduce me in the back of a limousine before, either.' Golden eyes rested on her intently and then, abruptly, he took his attention off her again. 'I don't think you'll find Dr Scipione too officious. He believes that time heals all.' He strolled back to the door, lithe as a leopard on the prowl. 'Bernardo's wife will come up and help you to get into bed.'

'I don't need——'

'Catherine,' he interrupted, 'one of the minor advantages of being my wife is being waited on hand and foot, thus saving your energy for more important pursuits.'

Her eyes danced. 'And one of the major ones?'

Hooded dark eyes wandered at a leisurely pace over her, and heat pooled in her pelvis, her stomach clenching. 'I'll leave that to your imagination, active as I know it to be. *Buona sera, cara.* I'll see you tomorrow.'

'Tomorrow?' She sat up in shock.

'Rest and peace.' Luc made the reminder mockingly and shut the door.

She stared up at the elaborately draped canopy above her. You were flirting with him, a little voice said. What was so strange about that? She couldn't ever recall doing it before. As a rule, she guarded and picked and chose her words with Luc in much the same fashion as one trod a careful passage round a sleeping volcano. Only at the beginning had she been naïve enough to blurt out exactly what was on her mind.

But she wasn't conscious of that barrier now, hadn't been all day or even last night. She was no longer in awe of Luc. When had that happened? Presumably some time during this past year. And yet Luc had said he had never seen her like this in a long time. What was this? This, she conceded, hugging a pillow dripping lace and ribbons to her fast-beating heart, was being wonderfully, madly and utterly without restraint . . . happy.

CHAPTER FIVE

THE rails of clothing in the dressing-room bedazzled Catherine. Encouraged, the little maid, Guilia, pressed back more doors: day-wear, evening-wear, leisure-wear, shelves of cobwebby, gorgeous lingerie and row upon row of shoes, everything grouped into tiny bands of colour. Co-ordination for the non-colour-clever woman, she thought dazedly. Luc had bought her an entire new wardrobe.

Such an extensive collection could not have been put together overnight. Overwhelming as the idea was, she could only see one viable explanation—Luc must have been planning to bring her to Italy for months! As her fingertips lingered on a silk dress, Guilia looked anxious and swung out a full-length gown, contriving to be very apologetic about the suggested exchange.

'*Grazie*, Guilia.'

'*Prego, signorina.*' With enthusiasm, Guilia whipped out lingerie and shoes and carried the lot reverently through to the bedroom. Catherine recognised a plant when she saw one. Guilia was here to educate her in the nicest possible way on what to wear for every possible occasion. Luc excelled on detail. Guilia had probably been programmed to bar the wardrobe doors if presented with a pretty cabbage-rose print.

It was eight in the evening. She had slept the clock round, slumbering through her first day at Castelleone. Last night, Bernardo's wife, Francesca, had fussed her into bed with the warmth of a mother hen. Dr Scipione had then made his début, a rotund little man with a pronounced resemblance to Santa Claus and an expression of soulful understanding.

Only when he had gone had she realised that she had chattered her head off the whole time he was there. He had only made her uneasy once by saying, 'Sometimes the mind forgets because it wants to forget. It shuts a door in self-protection.'

'What would I want to protect myself from?' she laughed.

'Ask yourself what you most fear and there may well lie the answer. It could be that when you fully confront that fear your mind will unlock that door,' he suggested. 'I suspect that you are not ready for that moment as yet.'

What did she most fear? Once it had been losing Luc, but since Luc had asked her to marry him that old insecurity had been banished forever. And the truth was that a little hiccup in her memory-banks did not currently have the power to alarm her—despite a nagging anxiety which she resolutely banished.

Attired in the fitting cerise-hued sheath, which was tighter over the fullness of her breasts than Guilia seemed to have expected, judging by the speed with which she had whipped out a tape-measure, Catherine sat down at the magnificent Gothic-styled dressing-table and smiled at the familiarity of the jewellery on display there. Her watch, stamped with the date she had first met Luc; clasping it to her wrist, she marvelled at how long it seemed since she had worn it. A leather box disclosed a slender diamond necklace and drop earrings; a second, a shimmering delicate bracelet. Christmas in Switzerland and her birthday, she reflected dreamily.

Leaving the bedroom, she peered over the stone balcony of the vast circular gallery. Bernardo's bald-spot was visible in the hall far below. She hurried downstairs and said in halting Italian, '*Buona sera*, Bernardo. *Dov'é* Signor Santini?'

Bernardo looked anguished. He wrung his hands and muttered something inaudible. Abruptly she turned, her eyes widening. Raised voices had a carrying quality in the echoing spaces around them.

One of the doors stood ajar. A tall black-haired woman, with shoulder-pads that put new meaning into power-dressing, was ranting, presumably at Luc, who was out of view. Or was she pleading? It was hard to tell.

Catherine tensed. She had no difficulty in recognising Rafaella Peruzzi. She was the only person Catherine knew who could argue with Luc and still have a job at the end of the day. She inhabited a nebulous grey area in Luc's life, somewhere between old friend and employee. She was also Santini Electronics' most efficient hatchet-woman. She lived, breathed, ate and slept profit . . . and Luc.

She had grown up with him. She had modelled herself on him. She was tough, ruthless and absolutely devoted to his interests. At some stage she had also shared a bed with Luc. Nobody had told Catherine that. Nobody had needed to tell her. Rafaella was a piece of Luc's past, but the past was a hopeful present in her eyes every time she looked at him. The women who blazed a quickly forgotten trail through his bedroom didn't bother Rafaella. Catherine had.

'You've got six weeks left. Enjoy him while you can,' she had derided the first time Catherine met her. 'With Luc, it never lasts longer than three months, and, with the clothes-sense you've got, honey, another six weeks should be quite a challenge for him.'

Luc was talking very quietly now. Rafaella vented a strangled sob and spat back in staccato Italian. Catherine moved away, ashamed that she hadn't moved sooner, and uneasily certain of the source of the drama. Yesterday, Luc had publicly announced his marital plans. Rafaella was reeling. Her pain seared Catherine with a strange sister pain. There but for the grace of God go I.

Luc was the sun round which Rafaella revolved. She could not resist that pull even when it scorched her; she could not break free. Though she knew that she was overstepping the boundaries that Luc set, she would still interfere. That was Rafaella. Stubborn, persistent, remorseless in enmity. Sometimes what disturbed Catherine most about Rafaella was her similarity to Luc. By the law of averages, she had thought uneasily more than once, Luc and Rafaella ought to have been a match made in heaven.

A door slammed on its hinges with an almighty crash. Bernardo had made himself scarce. Catherine wasn't quick enough. Rafaella stalked across the hall and circled her like a killer shark drawn by a lump of raw meat, rage and hatred splintering from her diamond-hard stare.

'You bitch!' She launched straight into attack. 'He wouldn't believe me when I told him, but I'll be back when I can prove it. And when I get the evidence you'll be out with the garbage, because he'll never forgive you!'

'Rafaella.' Luc was poised fifty feet away, lithe and sleek as a panther about to spring, his features savagely set.

She shot him a fierce, embittered glance. 'I wanted a closer look at the only truly honest woman you've ever met! She must be on the endangered species list. And, *caro*,' she forecast on her passage to the door, 'you're in for a severe dose of indigestion.'

Bernardo reappeared out of nowhere and surged to facilitate her exit. Catherine slowly breathed again. Rafaella, out of control and balked of her prey, was an intimidating experience. And she was astounded by her threats. What wouldn't Luc believe? What did Rafaella intend to prove? What would Luc never forgive her for?

'What on earth was she talking about?' she whispered tautly.

Smouldering tension still vibrated from Luc. She could read nothing in the steady beat of his dark eyes. For an instant it seemed to her that that stare both probed and challenged, but she dismissed the idea when a faintly sardonic smile lighted his expression. 'Nothing that need concern you.'

But it *did* concern her, she reasoned frustratedly as he curved a possessive arm to her slim shoulders and guided her into the magnificently proportioned *salone*. 'And Rafaella need not concern you either,' he completed.

'Why?' she prompted uncertainly.

'As of now, she no longer works for me,' Luc drawled with a chilling lack of sentiment.

Catherine was immediately filled with guilt. Rafaella lived for her career. If she hadn't been hanging about in the hall, the incident which had so enraged Luc would never have occurred. 'She was terribly upset, Luc. Shouldn't you make allowances for that?' she muttered after a long pause, resenting the ironic twist of fate that had set her up as the brunette's sole defender.

'What is wrong with you?' Luc demanded, abrasive in his incredulity. 'In the same position, she'd slit your throat without a second's hesitation. She walks into my home, she insults me, she insults you... and you expect me to take that lying down? I don't believe this!'

'She lost her head and it wouldn't have happened if... if...' she fumbled awkwardly beneath his piercing scrutiny '... she didn't love you.'

'Love like that I can do without,' he responded, unmoved.

'Sometimes,' she whispered, 'you can be very unfeeling, Luc.'

His superb bone-structure clenched, something more than irritation leaping through him now. 'Which translates to a ruthless, insensitive bastard, does it not?' he sizzled back at her.

Nobody criticised Luc. Rafaella might argue with him, but she would not have dreamt of criticising him. From being an infant prodigy in a very ordinary, poorly educated family in awe of his intellectual gifts, Luc had stalked into early adulthood, unfettered by any need or demand to consider anyone but himself. But he was in the wrong and she was helplessly tempted to tell him that plainly, had to bite back the words. He could not treat Rafaella as an old friend one moment and a humble employee the next. It had not been a kindness to keep Rafaella so close when he was aware of her feelings for him. It had only encouraged her to hope.

'I didn't say that,' she said tightly. 'Don't shout me down.'

'I am not shouting you down. You fascinate me. You belong up on a cloud with a harp!' he derided with acid bite. 'You haven't the slightest conception of what makes other human beings tick.'

Catherine lifted her chin. 'I only said that Rafaella deserves a little compassion——'

'Compassion? If you were bleeding to death by the side of the road, she'd sell tickets!' he grated. 'She's out because I don't trust her any more. I understand her too well. The first opportunity she gets, she'll stick a knife in your back, even if it costs her everything she has.'

Her flesh chilled involuntarily at the deadly certainty with which he voiced that belief.

'The subject is now closed. Are you coming to dinner?' he concluded drily.

'Will you give her a reference?'

There was a sharp little silence. Luc spun back, clashed with the hauntingly beautiful blue eyes pinned expectantly to him. '*Per amor di Dio* . . . all right, if that's what you want!' he gritted, out of all patience.

He wasn't built to recognise compromise. Compromise was a retrograde step towards losing, and losing didn't come gracefully to Luc. Catherine tucked into her dinner with unblemished appetite. Luc poked at his appetiser, complained about the temperature of the wine, sat tapping his fingers in tyrannical tattoo between courses and cooled down only slowly.

'What did you think of Dr Scipione?' he enquired over the coffee.

'He was very kind. Is he the local doctor?'

An ebony brow quirked. 'He lives in Rome. He's also one of the world's leading authorities on amnesia.'

'Oh.' Catherine almost choked on her dismay. 'I treated him as if he was just anybody!'

'Catherine, one of your greatest virtues is the ability to treat everyone from the lowliest cleaning-lady up in exactly the same way,' he murmured, unexpectedly linking his fingers with hers, a smile curving the formerly hard line of his lips. 'Let us at least agree that your manners are a great deal better than mine. By the way, I have some papers for you to sign before we can get married. We should take care of them now.'

She accompanied him into the library where he had been with Rafaella earlier. It was packed with books from floor to ceiling, and a massive desk sat before the tall windows. Fierce discomfiture gripped her when she saw the sheaf of documents he lifted. Forms to fill in...bureaucracy. With Luc present, her worst nightmare had full substance.

'This is the...' Luc handed her a pen but she didn't absorb his explanation. There was a thunderbeat of tension in her ears. 'You sign here.' A brown forefinger indicated the exact spot and stayed there.

The paper was a grey and white blur. Covertly she bent her head. 'I just s-sign?' she stammered, terrified that there was something else to do that he wasn't mentioning because he would naturally assume that she could easily see it and read it for herself.

'You just sign.'

She inscribed her signature slowly and carefully. Luc whipped the document away and presented her with a second. 'And here.'

More hurriedly, less carefully, she complied. 'Is that it?' Struggling to conceal her relief at his nod of confirmation, she lifted the document. 'You once told me never to sign anything I couldn't read,' she joked unsteadily.

'I was more obtuse than I am now.' He studied her. The strain etched in her delicate profile was beginning to ease but her hand was shaking perceptibly. 'It's in Italian, *cara*,' he told her very gently.

'I wasn't really looking at it.' Clumsily she put it down again.

Before she could turn away, lean hands came down to rest on her tense shoulders, keeping her in front of him where he lounged on the edge of the polished desk. 'I believe it's more than that,' he countered quietly. 'Don't you think it's time that we stopped playing this game? Whether you realise it or not, it's caused a lot of misunderstanding between us.'

Her face had gone chalk-white. 'G-game?'

He sighed. 'Why do you think I choose your meals for you when we dine out?'

'I . . . I dither; it saves time,' she muttered, making an abrupt move to walk away, but he was impervious to the hint.

'And I'm just naturally insensitive to what you might choose for yourself?' he chided. 'Catherine, I've been aware that you have trouble reading since the first week

GET A FREE TEDDY BEAR...

You'll love this plush, cuddly Teddy Bear, an adorable accessory for your dressing table, bookcase or desk. Measuring 5½" tall, he's soft and brown and has a bright red ribbon around his neck—he's completely captivating! And he's yours *absolutely free*, when you accept this no-risk offer!

AND FOUR FREE BOOKS!

Here's a chance to get **four free Harlequin Presents® novels** from the Harlequin Reader Service®—so you can see for yourself that we're like **no ordinary book club!**

We'll send you four free books...but you never have to buy anything or remain a member any longer than you choose. You could even accept the free books and cancel immediately. In that case, you'll owe nothing and be under **no obligation!**

Find out for yourself why thousands of readers enjoy receiving books by mail from the Harlequin Reader Service. They like the **convenience of home delivery...** they like getting the best new novels months before they're available in bookstores...and they love our **discount prices!**

Try us and see! Return this card promptly. We'll send your free books and a free Teddy Bear, under the terms explained on the back. We hope you'll want to remain with the reader service— but the choice is always yours!

306 CIH AJA7 (C-H-P-05/93)

▼ CLAIM YOUR FREE BOOKS AND FREE GIFT! RETURN THIS CARD TODAY! ▶

NO OBLIGATION TO BUY!

I spent with you in London. I saw through all those painfully elaborate little stratagems and, I have to admit, I was pretty shocked.'

Her stricken gaze veiled as tears lashed her eyelids in a blistering surge. She wanted the ground to open up and swallow her. His deep voice, no matter how calm and quiet it was, stung like a whip on her most vulnerable skin. Her throat was convulsing and she couldn't speak. All she wanted to do was get away from him, but his arms banded round her slim waist like steel hawsers.

'We are going to have this all out in the open,' Luc informed her steadily. 'Why didn't you tell me right at the beginning that you were dyslexic? I didn't realise that. You were ashamed of it and I didn't want to hurt your feelings, so I pretended as well. I ignored it but, in my ignorance of the true situation, I hoped very much that you would do something about it.'

'I can't!' she gasped. 'They did all they could for me at school but I'll never be able to read properly!'

'Do you think I don't know that now? Will you stop trying to get away from me?' he demanded, subduing her struggles with determined hands. 'I know that you're dyslexic, but I didn't know it then. I thought——'

'You thought I was just illiterate!' she sobbed in agonised interruption. 'I'll never forgive you for doing this to me!'

'You're going to listen to me.' He held her fast. 'I was at fault as well. I took the easy way out. What I didn't like, I chose not to see. I should have tried to help you myself. Had I done that, I would have realised what was really wrong. But you should have told me,' he censured.

'Let go of me!' she railed at him, shaken by tempestuous sobs of humiliation.

'Don't you understand what I'm trying to tell you?' He gave her a fierce little shake that momentarily roused her from her distress. 'If I had known, if I had under-

stood, I wouldn't have been angry when you made no
effort to improve your situation! I'm not getting through
to you, am I?'

'You're ashamed of me!' she accused him despairingly.

Sliding upright, he crushed her into his arms and laced
one hand into the golden fall of her hair to tip her head
back. 'No, I'm not,' he contradicted fiercely. 'There is
nothing to be ashamed of. Einstein was dyslexic, da Vinci
was dyslexic. If it was good enough for them, it's good
enough for you!'

'Oh, Luc!' A laugh somewhere between a hiccup and
a sob escaped her as she looked up at him. 'Good
enough? I probably have it worse than they did.'

'I don't know how I could have been so blind for so
long,' he admitted. 'You have no sense of direction, you
can't tell left from right, the tying of a bow defeats you,
and sometimes you're just a little forgetful.' There was
a teasing, soothing quality to that concluding statement.

She was still shaking. Her distress had been too great
to ebb quickly. She buried her face in his jacket, weak
and uncertain, but beyond that there was this glorious
sense of release from a pretence that had frequently
lacerated her nerves and kept her in constant fear of
discovery.

'You don't mind, you really don't mind?' she
muttered.

'All that I mind is that you didn't trust me enough to
tell me yourself, but, now I know, we can speak to an
educational specialist—I'm sure you can be helped.'
Tipping her head back, he produced a hanky and auto-
matically mopped her up, smiling down at her, and
something about that smile made her heart skip an entire
beat. 'It wasn't brave to suffer in silence, it was foolish.
I would have understood your difficulties. We live in a
world in which the capacity to interpret the written word

is taken for granted. How did you manage to work in the art gallery? I've often wondered that,' he confided.

'Elaine taped the catalogue for me.'

He finger-combed her hair back into a semblance of order. 'Secrets,' he said, 'create misunderstandings.'

'That's the only one I have,' she sighed. 'You're always tidying me up and putting me back together again.'

'Maybe I enjoy doing it. Have you thought of that?' he teased, his husky voice fracturing slightly as she stared up at him.

All the oxygen in the air seemed to be used up without warning. Desire clutched at her stomach in a lancing surge. Her breasts felt constrained within their silken covering as her sensitive flesh swelled and her nipples peaked into tight aching buds. The sensations were blindingly physical, unnervingly powerful, and she trembled.

He withdrew his hand from her hair and stepped back. 'It's late. You should go to bed,' he muttered harshly. 'If you don't, I'll take you here.'

A heady flush lit her cheeks. She backed away obediently on cotton-wool legs. She couldn't drag her eyes from his dark-golden beauty. The view was spiced by her intrinsic awareness of the savage sexual intensity contained below that surface calm and control. She wanted him. She wanted him so much that it scared her. In her memory there was nothing to equal the force of the hunger she was experiencing now. It confused her, embarrassed her.

'I'm expecting an important call,' he added, and, as she looked at him in surprise, said succinctly, 'Time zones.'

She couldn't picture Luc sitting up to take a phone call, no matter how important it was. People called at his convenience, not their own. Still watching him, she found the door more by accident than design and fumbled it open. 'I really am feeling marvellous,' she assured him in a self-conscious rush before she ducked out into the hall.

Although she had bathed earlier, Catherine decided to have a refreshing shower. Fifteen minutes later, liberally anointed with some of the scented essences she had found on a shelf in the *en suite* bathroom, she donned the diaphanous peach silk nightdress lying across the bed and slid between the sheets to lie back in a breathless state of anticipation and wait for Luc.

The minutes dragged past. She amused herself by thinking lovingly of how reassuring he had been about her dyslexia. He was right. She should have confided in him a long time ago. He would have understood. She saw that now, regretted her silence and subterfuge, and felt helplessly guilty about misjudging him so badly.

Somewhere in the midst of these ruminations, she dozed off and dreamt. It was the strangest dream. She was writing on a mirror, sound-spelling 'Ah-ree-va'...and she was crying while she did it, reflections of what she was writing and her own unhappy face making the task all the more difficult. There was so much pain in that image that she wanted to scream with it, and she woke up with a start in the darkness, tears wet on her cheeks.

Somebody had switched the light out. She made that connection, bridging the gap between a piece of the past she had forgotten and the present. She slumped back against the pillows, clinging to the dream, but there was so little of it to hold on to and build on. It was the pain she recalled most, a bewildered, frantic sense of pain and defeat.

Padding into the bathroom, she splashed her face and dried it. Who had switched the light off? It must have been Luc. He had come to her and she had been fast asleep. She lifted a weak hand to her forehead where the pounding in her temples was only slowly steadying. It was impossible to stifle a sudden, desperate, tearing need to be with him.

She approached the door in her bedroom which she assumed connected with his. Finding it locked, she frowned and crept out on to the gallery, dimly wondering what time it was. The bedroom itself was in darkness when she entered, but a triangle of light was spilling from the open bathroom door. She could hear a shower running and she smiled. It couldn't be that late. She scrambled into the turned-back bed as quietly as a mouse.

The shower went off and the light almost simultaneously. A second or two later the bedroom curtains were drawn back. Luc unlatched one of the windows and stood there in the moonlight, magnificently naked, towelling his hair dry.

He was asking to catch his death of cold but the urge to announce her presence dwindled. Whipcord muscles flexed taut beneath the smooth golden skin of his back. Her mouth ran dry. Feeling mortifyingly like a voyeur, she closed her eyes. The mattress gave slightly with his weight and three-quarters of the sheet was wrenched from her.

As he rolled over, punching a pillow and narrowly missing her head, he came into sudden contact with her. '*Dio!*' Jerking semi-upright, he lunged at the light above the bed before she could prevent him.

One hand braced tautly on the carved headboard, he stared down at her in shock. 'Catherine?'

She could feel one of those ghastly beetroot blushes crawling in a tide over her exposed skin. Somehow his tone implied that the very last place he expected to find her was in his bed. 'I couldn't sleep.'

He slid lower on the mattress, surveying her intently, his cheekbones harshly accentuated. 'No more could I. Come here.' He reached out with a determined hand and brought her close, not giving her time to respond to what was more of a command than a request. 'I want you,' he admitted roughly. 'Do you have any idea how much I want you?'

'I'm here,' she whispered, suddenly shy of him.

Bending his dark head, he muttered something ferocious in Italian and crushed her lips apart with a savage urgency that took her very much by surprise. His tongue ravished the tender interior of her mouth. She might have been a life-saving draught to a male driven to the edge of madness by thirst. He bruised her lips and drank deep and long until her head swam and she couldn't breathe. Fire as elemental as he was leapt through her veins.

Her hands found his shoulders. He was burning up as though he had a fever, his skin hot and dry, his long, hard body savagely tense against hers. Lean fingers fumbled with an unusual lack of dexterity at the silk that concealed her from him. With a stifled growl of frustration, he drew back and tore the whisper-fine fabric apart with impatient hands.

'Luc!' Catherine surfaced abruptly from a drowning well of passion and fixed shocked eyes on him as he knelt over her, trailing the torn remnants from her and tossing them carelessly aside. As she made an instinctive attempt to cover herself from his devouring scrutiny, he caught at her wrists and flattened them to the bed.

'Please.' It was a word he very rarely employed and there was a note in that roughened plea that stabbed at her heart and made her ache.

Brilliant golden eyes ran over her in a look as physical as touch, exploring the burgeoning swell of her breasts, the smoothness of her narrow ribcage, the feminine curve of her hips and the soft curls at the juncture of her thighs.

'Squisita...perfetta,' he muttered raggedly as he drew her towards him, and his mouth swooped down to capture a taut nipple.

Her back arched as a whimper of formless sound was torn from her throat. He suckled her tender flesh with an intensely erotic enjoyment that drove her wild. He bit with subtle delicacy, his hand toying with the neglected twin, shaping, tugging, exciting until she was writhing beneath his ministrations. She wanted his weight on her and he denied her, lifting his head only to trail the tip of his tongue teasingly down between her breasts, traversing the pale skin of her ribs and dipping into the hollow of her navel.

Her hands dug into his hair and tightened in immediate protest as he strung a line of wholly determined kisses from the bend of her knee to the smooth inner skin of her thigh, tensing tiny muscles she didn't know she possessed. And then her neck extended and her head fell back on the pillows. A cry fled her lips, all thought arrested as she sank into the seduction of pure sensation and was lost in the frantic clamour of her own body.

At the peak of an excitement more of agony than pleasure, Catherine cried out his name, and his hands curved hard to her hips as he rose above her, silencing her with the tormenting force of his mouth. Against her most tender flesh, he was hot and insistent. For a split second he stared down at her, desire and demand stamped in his dark, damp features, and then he moved, thrusting deep as a bolt of lightning rending the heavens.

Pain clenched her, unexpected enough to dredge her briefly from the driving, all-enveloping hunger for satisfaction that he had induced. He stilled, dealt her a look in which tenderness and triumph blazed, more blatant than speech, and pressed a fleeting benediction of a kiss to her brow. He muttered something about doubting her and never doubting her again.

She was in no condition to absorb what he was saying. With tiny, subtle, circling movements of his hips, he was inciting her to passion again, accustoming her to his fullness. All conscious thought was suspended. She was lost in the primal rhythm of giving all and taking everything, driven mindless and powerless towards that final shattering release. When it came in wave after wave of unbelievable pleasure, it was sublime.

His harsh groan of masculine satisfaction still echoing in her ears, she let her hands rove possessively over his sweat-dampened skin. Obtrusive questions licked at the corners of her mind. Had it ever been that profound, that overwhelming before? She remembered excitement, but not an excitement that swept her so quickly into oblivion. She remembered his hunger, but not a hunger that threatened to rage out of control in its raw intensity. She remembered the sweet joy of fulfilment, but not a fulfilment that stole her very soul with its fiery potency.

And she also remembered . . . sadly . . . that Luc was invariably halfway to the shower by now, shunning with that essential detachment of his the aftermath of passion when she had so desperately wanted him to stay in her arms.

He was holding her now as if at any moment she might make a break for freedom, and the awareness provoked a deep rush of tenderness within her. She rubbed her cheek lovingly against a strong brown shoulder. He shifted languorously like a sleek cat stretching beneath a caress, as unashamedly physical in his enjoyment as any member of the animal kingdom.

'I had a very strange dream.' She broke the silence hesitantly, afraid that the magic might escape. 'I don't know if it was a memory.'

Tension snaked through his relaxed length. 'What was it?'

'You'll probably laugh.'

'I promise I won't. Tell me.'

'I was writing on a mirror,' she whispered. 'Can you imagine that? I never write anything but my name unless I can help it, and there I was, writing on this mirror!'

'Amazing,' he murmured softly.

'It wasn't. It felt scary,' she muttered, half under her breath. 'It probably has nothing to do with my memory at all. What do you think?'

'I think you're talking too much.' Rolling over, he carried her with him on to a cool spot on the bed. 'And I would much rather make love, *bella mia.*' He nipped teasingly at the velvet-soft lobe of her ear and forged an erotic path along the slender arch of her throat as she involuntarily extended it for his pleasure. Her hair splayed out across the pillow and he studied the chopped ends wryly and looked down at her. 'You've been using scissors to hack at your hair again.'

'I can't think why,' she confessed with a slight frown. 'I'll go and get it cut tomorrow.'

'Someone can come here to take care of it,' he countered.

'I want to see Rome.'

'Bumper-to-bumper traffic and unbelievable heat and noise and pollution. Not to mention the tourists.' He extracted a long lingering kiss before she could protest, and then he started to make love to her again. This time he was incredibly gentle and seductive, utilising every art to enthrall her. Pleasure piled on pleasure in layers of ever-deepening delight. Incredibly, it was even more exciting than the first time.

A single white rose lay on the pillow when she opened her eyes. She discovered it by accident, her hand feeling blindly across the bed in automatic search for Luc. Instead she found a thorn and, with a yelp, she reared up, sucking her pricked finger. And there it was. The rose. She wanted to cry, but that was soppy. The dew still dampened the petals. She tried to picture her supremely elegant Luc clambering through a rosebed and failed utterly. A gardener had undoubtedly done the clambering. Luc wouldn't be caught dead in a flowerbed. All the same, it was the thought which counted and, for an unromantic guy, he really was trying very hard to please. In the end, it was that reflection rather than the rose that flooded her eyes with tears.

CHAPTER SIX

THE heat had reduced Catherine to a somnolent languor. She heard footsteps, recognised them. The cool of a large parasol blocked out the sun and shadowed her. She turned her head, rested her chin on her elbow and watched Luc sink down on the edge of the lounger beside her. In an open-necked short-sleeved white shirt and fitting black jeans that accentuated slim hips and long, lean thighs, he looked stunning enough to stop an avalanche in its tracks. A sun-dazed smile tilted her soft lips. He also looked distinctly short-tempered.

Since wedding fervour had hit Castelleone, the peace, the privacy and the perfect organisation which Luc took for granted had been swept away by a chattering tidal wave of caterers and florists and constantly shrilling phones. Luc's enthusiasm had waned with almost comical speed once he'd realised what throwing a reception for several hundred people entailed.

'I feel like throwing them all out,' he admitted grimly.

'You wanted a big splash,' she reminded him with more truth than tact.

'I thought it was what you expected!' he condemned.

'A couple of witnesses and a bunch of flowers would have done me,' she confided, feeling too warm and lazy to choose her words.

He threw up expressive hands. 'Now she tells me!'

The rattle of ice in glasses interrupted them. Luc leapt up and carefully intercepted Bernardo before he could come any closer. Catherine absorbed this defensive exercise with hidden amusement. Anyone would have been

forgiven for thinking that her bare back was the equivalent of indecent exposure. Yesterday, a low-flying light
plane had provoked an embargo on topless sunbathing
and a no doubt fierce complaint to the local airfield.
She wondered why it had taken her all this time to notice
just how shockingly old-fashioned Luc could be about
some things.

He cast her a sardonic glance. 'I love the way you lie
out here as though there's nothing happening.'

'Bernardo knows exactly what he's doing.' With an
excess of tact, she did not add that if Luc stopped wading
in to interfere and organise, imbuing everyone with the
feeling that their very best wasn't good enough, the last-
minute arrangements would be proceeding a lot more
smoothly. Having given the intimidating impression that
he intended to supervise and criticise every little detail,
he was not receiving a moment's peace.

Tomorrow, she reflected blissfully. Tomorrow, she
would be Luc's wife. The 'died and gone to heaven' sensation embraced her again. Whole days had slid away
in a haze of hedonistic pleasure since her arrival in Italy.
Never had she enjoyed such utter relaxation and self-
indulgence. Her sole contribution to the wedding had
been two dress-fittings. Her gown, fashioned of exquisite handmade lace, was gorgeous. It was wonderful
what could be achieved at short notice if you had as
much money as Luc had.

'Tomorrow, I'll be rich,' she mused absently.

After an arrested pause, Luc flung back his gleaming
dark head and roared with laughter. 'You're probably
the only woman in the world who would dare to say that
to me *before* the wedding.'

She gave him an abstracted smile. Luc? Luc was wonderful, fantastic, beautiful, incredible, divine... With
unwittingly expressive eyes pinned to him, she ran out
of superlatives, and he sent her a glittering look that

made her toes curl. That detachment which had once frozen her out when she got too close was steadily becoming a feature of the past.

Last night, Luc had actually talked about his family. And he never talked about them. The death of his parents and sister in that plane crash had shattered him but he had never actually come close to admitting that fact before. And she was quite certain that he would never admit the guilt he had suppressed when they died. On the rise to the top, Luc had left his family behind.

He had given them luxury, but not the luxury of himself. Business had always come first. He had sent them off on an expensive vacation in apology for yet another cancelled visit and he had never seen them alive again. When he had talked about them last night, it had been one of those confiding conversations that he could only bring himself to share with forced casualness in the cloaking darkness of the bedroom. Until now, she had never understood just how very difficult it was for Luc to express anything which touched him deeply.

Sliding up on her knees, she lifted her bikini top. His dark eyes travelled in exactly the direction she had known they would, lingering on the unbound curves briefly revealed. A heady pink fired her cheeks but, as she arched her back to do up the fastener, the all-male intensity of his appraisal roused an entirely feminine satisfaction as old as Eve within her.

'You like me looking at you,' he commented, lazily amused.

She bent her head, losing face and confidence. 'You're not supposed to notice that.'

'I can't help noticing it when you look so smug.'

Leaning lithely forward, he scooped her bodily across the divide between the loungers with that easy strength of his that melted her somewhere deep down inside. He laced an idle hand into her hair and claimed her mouth

in a provocative sensual exploration. The world lurched
violently on its axis and went into a spin, leaving her
light-headed and weak. It didn't matter how often he
touched her, it was always the same. There had always
been this between them, this shatteringly physical bond.

And once it had scared her. In her innocence, she had
believed it one-sided, had assumed that Luc could, if he
wanted, discover the same pleasure with any other
woman. She was not so quick to make that assumption
now. In the long passion-drenched hours which had
turned night into day and day into night, the depth of
Luc's hunger had driven her again and again to the brink
of exhaustion.

He released her mouth with reluctance. 'You make me
insatiable.' The sexy growl to that lancing confession did
nothing to cool her fevered blood and she rested her head
on his shoulder. 'Somehow, I doubt,' he murmured, 'that
it'll take that long for you to become pregnant.'

'Pregnant?' she squeaked, jerking back from him, her
first reaction one of shock and, curiously, fear.

His hands steadied her before she could overbalance
and he nuzzled his lips hotly into the hollow of her collarbone where a tiny pulse beat out her tension. 'Don't
tell me you believed in the stork story,' he teased. 'Believe it or not, what we've been doing in recent days does
have another more basic purpose above and beyond mere
pleasure.'

She was trembling. 'Yes, but——'

'And we haven't been taking any steps to forestall such
a result,' he reminded her with complete calm.

That awareness was only hitting Catherine now. It
shook her that a matter which had once been shrouded
with such importance could have slipped her mind so
entirely. There had been no contraceptive pills in her
possession. Evidently she was no longer taking them.
Remembering to take them had once been the bane of

her existence, invoking horrid attacks of panic when she realised that she had forgotten one or two. If Luc realised just how many near misses they had had, he would probably feel very much as she did now.

That background hadn't prepared her very well for Luc's smoothly talking about having a baby as if it was the most natural thing in the world. Which of course it was...if you were married. In the circumstances, she decided that her initial sense of panic at his comment had been quite understandable. Where reproduction was concerned, she had to learn a whole new way of thinking.

Seemingly impervious to the frantic readjustments he had set in train, Luc ran a caressing hand down her spine and eased her closer. 'Didn't you notice that omission?' he said softly.

'No,' she muttered with instinctive guilt.

'I want children while I'm young enough to enjoy them.'

It crossed her mind that he might just have mentioned that before taking the decision right over her head, as it were. But equally fast came a seductive image of carrying Luc's baby and she was overcome by the prospect and quite forgot to be annoyed with him. 'Yes,' she agreed wistfully.

Engaged on cutting a sensual path across her fine-boned shoulder, Luc murmured huskily, 'I knew you'd agree with me. Now, instead of rushing to look into every baby carriage that passes by, you can concentrate on your own.'

'Do I do that?' she whispered.

'You do,' he said wryly.

Once anything to do with babies had left Luc arctic-cold. Naturally she couldn't help but be surprised that he should want a child with such immediacy. But when she thought about it for a minute or two, it began to make sense. Luc was entering marriage much as he en-

tered a business deal, armed with expectations. He
wanted an heir, that was all. You couldn't empire-build
without a dynasty. But still she couldn't summon a smile
to her face and she couldn't shake off that irrational fear
assailing her.

Common sense ought to have reasoned it away. She
loved Luc. She loved children. Where was the problem?
Yet still the feeling persisted and her temples began to
throb. When the phone buzzed on the table and Luc
reached for it impatiently, she was starting to feel distinctly shaky and sick into the bargain.

Luc was talking in Japanese with the languid cool of
someone fluent in a dozen languages. A frown pleating
his dark brows, he sighed as he replaced the phone.
'Business,' he said. 'I have to go inside to make a few
calls. I'll be as quick as I can.'

Sunlight played blindingly on the surface of the pool
several feet away. As a faint breeze sent a glimmering
tide of ripples across the water, the effect was almost
hynotic. Catherine's head ached too much to think. She
wondered ruefully if she had had too much sun.

A sound jerked her out of an uneasy doze. A child
emerged from below the trees. His stubby little legs
pumped energetically in pursuit of the ball he was
chasing. As it headed directly for the water, Catherine
flew upright, consumed by alarm. But he caught the ball
before it reached the edge, and as he did so one of the
maids came racing down the slope from the castle.

'*Scusi, signorina, scusi!*' she gasped in frantic apology
for the intrusion as she scooped the child up into her
arms. He gave a wail of protest. As he was hurried away,
still clutching his ball, Catherine stopped breathing.

The thumping behind her forehead had for a split
second become unbearable, but now it receded. She
didn't even notice the fact. She was in a benumbed state
that went beyond shock into incredulous horror.

Daniel . . . Daniel! The sybaritic luxury of the pool with its marble surround vanished as she unfroze.

Snatching up the phone, she pressed the button for the internal house line. A secretary answered. 'This is Miss Parrish.' She had to cough to persuade her voice to grow from a thread into comprehensible volume. 'I want you to get me a number in England and connect me. It's urgent,' she stressed, straining to recall Peggy's maiden name and the address of her home and finally coming up with them.

Shaking like the victim of an accident, she sat down before her legs gave out beneath her. What sort of a mother could forget about her son? Oh, dear God, please let me wake up, please don't let this nightmare be real, she prayed with fervour.

The phone buzzed and she leapt at it.

'Hello? Hello?' Peggy was saying.

'It's Catherine. Is Daniel there?'

'He's out bringing in the hay. I cried off to make refreshments,' Peggy chattered. 'Our phone was out for a couple of days and we didn't realise. Have you been frantic, trying to get through?'

'Well——'

'I thought you would've been,' Peggy interrupted with her usual impatience. 'I tried to ring you a few times from the call-box in the village but I always struck out. I suppose you've been out scouring the pavements in search of a job if you've decided against working for Mrs Anstey.'

'I——'

'Daniel's having a fabulous time. The weather's been terrific. We were planning to camp out tonight but, of course, if you want to speak to him . . .'

'No, that's OK.' I've been kidnapped. I'm in Italy. I'm getting married tomorrow. The revelations went unspoken. Peggy would think she was a candidate for the funny farm. In any case, she would be home before they were back in London. Nobody need ever know, she thought in that first frantic flush of desperation.

'Catherine, somebody's just driven into the yard. Wow, fancy car. Can I ring you back?'

'No... no, I'm out... I mean, I'm ringing from somewhere else. Give my love to Daniel.' She dropped the phone as though it burnt, and tottered backwards on to the lounger.

The hideous, absolutely inexcusable events of the past week were suddenly all crowding in on her. She flinched and she shrank and she cringed over the replay. Humiliation scored letters of fire into her soul. From rock-bottom there was only one way to go, and that was up, as she relived what Luc had done to her.

And really, there wasn't anything that Luc *hadn't* done. While she was in no condition to know what was happening to her, he had moved in for the kill. Plotting and intrigue were a breath of fresh air to that Borgia temperament of his. It had been as easy as stealing candy from a baby. Baby. *Baby*! She blenched and recoiled from that terrifying train of thought, completely unable to deal with it on top of everything else.

For a week she had been unaware that she was living four years in the past. He had left nothing within her possession that might jog her memory. Not a newspaper or a television set or a calendar had been allowed anywhere within a mile of her.

Every detail had been bloodlessly, inhumanly precise. It had Luc stamped all over it. He hadn't made a single error. She had been baited, hooked and landed like a fish. Only even a fish would have had more sense of self-preservation. A fish wouldn't have scrambled up the line, thrown itself masochistically on to the gutting knife and looked forward to the heat of the grill... but she had.

What Luc wanted, he took. Scruples didn't come into it. Costs didn't come into it. The end result was all that interested him. He had believed that she had planned to marry Drew and, with Drew's freedom so close, time had been a luxury Luc hadn't had. No doubt if she had thrown herself gratefully at his feet that night marriage would never have been mentioned. But in resisting Luc, she had challenged Luc. And he could not resist a challenge.

Her teeth ground together and her stomach heaved. That degrading fish image wouldn't leave her alone. Her small hands clenched into fists. Rage shuddered through her; rage that knew no boundaries; rage so powerful that it boiled up in a violent physicality she had not known she could experience.

At that precise moment, Luc appeared, striding down the steps set into the slope, and she remembered the episode in the back of the limousine and death would have been too quick a release for him to satisfy her. Springing upright, she grabbed up a glass and threw it at him. As it smashed several feet to the left of him, he stilled.

'You filthy, rotten, cheating, conniving swine!' she railed at him, snatching up the second glass and hurling it with all her might. 'You rat!' she ranted, and the phone went in the same direction. 'You louse!' she launched, bending in a frenzy to take off a shoe, her rage only getting more out of control at her failure to hit a fixed target. 'Bastard!' She broke through her loathing for that particular word and punctuated it with her other shoe. 'I want to kill you!'

'Poison would be a better bet than a gun.' Luc spread a speaking glance over the far-flung positions of the missiles, entire and smashed. 'Marksmanship wouldn't appear to be one of your hidden talents.'

Her rage reached explosive, screaming proportions. 'Is that all you've got to say?'

'It seems fairly safe to assume that you've retrieved your memory,' he drawled. 'I'm not sure it would be safe to assume anything else.'

'No, it wouldn't be!' His complete cool was maddening her even more. 'If you were dying of thirst, I wouldn't give you a drink! If you were starving, I wouldn't feed you! If you were the only man left alive on this earth and I was the only woman, the human race would grind to a halt! You deserve to be horsewhipped and keelhauled and hung, and if I was a man I'd do it!'

'And if you were a man, you wouldn't be in this situation,' Luc input helpfully as she paused to catch her breath.

'I'm going to report you to the police!' Catherine blazed at him, satisfied to have at last found a realistic threat.

Luc angled his dark head back, piercing golden eyes resting on her. 'What for?'

'W-what for?' she stammered an octave higher. 'What for? You kidnapped me!'

'Did I drug you? Physically abuse you? Have you witnesses to these events?'

'I'll make it up; I'll lie!' she slashed back at him.

'But why did you stand so willingly at my side at the airport when I announced our marriage plans?' Luc enquired with the same immovable, incredibly outrageous cool.

'You've kept me a prisoner here all week!' In desperation, she set off on another tack, determined to nail him down to a crime on the statute books.

An ebony brow quirked. 'With locked doors? I don't recall refusing to let you go anywhere.'

'Physical abuse, then!' Catherine slung through gnashing teeth. 'I'll get you on that!'

Luc actually smiled. 'What physical abuse?'

Catherine drew herself up to her full five feet and one quarter inch and shrieked. 'You know very well what I'm talking about! While I...while I was not in my right mind, you took disgusting advantage of me!'

'Did I?' he murmured. 'Catherine, it is my considered opinion that over the past week you've been more in your right mind than you've been for almost five years.'

'How dare you?' she screamed at him, fit to be tied. 'How dare you say that to me?'

A broad shoulder shifted in an elegantly understated shrug. 'I say it because it is the truth.'

'The truth according to who?' she shouted ferociously. 'You take that back right now!'

'I have not the slightest intention of withdrawing that statement,' he informed her with careless provocation. 'When you calm down, you will realise that it is the truth.'

'When I calm down?' she yelled. 'Do I look like I'm about to calm down?'

Luc ran a reflective appraisal over her. 'If you could swim a little better, I would drop you in the pool.'

'You're not even sorry, are you?' That was one reality that was sinking in. It did nothing to reduce her fury.

He sighed. 'Why would I be sorry?'

'Why? Why?' She could hardly get the repetition out. 'Because I'm going to make you sorry! I should have known you wouldn't have a twinge of conscience about bringing me here!'

'You're quite right. I haven't.'

'You act as though I'm some sort of a thing, an object you can lift and lay at will!' As his wide mouth curled with amusement, she understood why people committed murder.

His lashes screened his expressive eyes. 'If you are an object to me, then I am an object to you in the same way.'

For a second she glared at him uncomprehendingly and then caught his meaning. 'I'm not talking about sex!' she raged.

'No,' he conceded. 'I had noticed that once the charge of physical abuse was withdrawn——'

'I didn't withdraw it!' she interrupted.

'You were careful to change the subject,' he countered. 'You want me every bit as much as I want you.'

'You conceited jerk! I was sick! I hate you!'

'You'll get over that,' he assured her.

'I'm not going to get over it! I'm leaving, walking out, departing...' she spelt out tempestuously.

'A fairly typical response of yours when the going threatens to get rough, but you're not doing a vanishing act this time.'

'I'm leaving you!' she shouted wildly.

'Watch the glass!' Luc raked at her rawly.

But it was too late. A sharp pain bit into her foot and she vented a gasp. Striding forward, Luc wrenched her off her feet, moved over to the nearest seat and literally tipped her up, a lean hand retaining a hold on one slender ankle. 'Stay still!' he roared at her. 'Or you'll push the glass in deeper.'

Sobbing with thwarted temper and pain, she let him withdraw the sliver and then she cursed him.

'I knew you would do that.'

'Let go of me!' she screeched.

'With all this broken glass around? You just have to be kidding,' he gibed, wrapping an immaculate hanky round her squirming foot. 'When did you last have a tetanus jab?'

'Six months ago!' she spat, infuriated beyond all bearing by the ignominy of her position. 'Did you hear what I said? I'm leaving!'

'Like hell you are.' Jerking up the sarong that had fallen on the ground, he proceeded to her utter disbelief to wrap it round her much as if she were a doll to be dressed.

She thrust his hands away. 'Don't you dare touch me! What do you mean—"Like hell you are"? You can't keep me here!'

Casting the sarong aside, he took her by surprise by lifting her and, when she fought tooth and nail with every limb flailing, he flung her over his shoulder.

'Let me go!' she shrieked, hammering at his back with her fists. 'What do you think you're doing?'

'Putting you under restraint for your own good. You're hysterical,' he bit out. 'And I've had enough.'

'*You've* had enough?' Her voice broke incredulously. 'Put me down!'

'*Sta' zitta.* Be quiet,' he ground out.

Gravity was threatening the bra of her bikini. She became more occupied with holding it in place than thumping any part of him she could reach. He was heading for the stone staircase that led up to the french doors on the first-floor gallery. 'I hate you!' she sobbed, tears of mortification, unvented fury and frustration flooding her eyes without warning.

A minute later Luc dumped her on her bed with about the same level of care as a sack of potatoes might have required. 'And hating me isn't making you happy, is it?' he breathed derisively. '*Per dio*, doesn't that tell you something?'

'That you're the most unscrupulous primitive I've ever come across!' she spat through her tears. 'And I'm leaving!'

'You're not going anywhere.'

'You can't stop me!' And you certainly can't make me marry you!' she asserted with returning confidence, wriggling off the bed and hobbling over to a chair to pull on the flimsy négligé lying there, suddenly feeling very exposed in what little there was of the bikini. 'And,

now that Drew's got his precious contract, you can't hold
that over me any more!'

'He signs for it one hour after the wedding.'

Catherine was paralysed in her tracks. Jerkily she
turned round. Shimmering golden eyes clashed with hers
in an almost physical assault. 'I had foreseen the possibility that this might occur.'

'He . . . he hasn't got it yet?' She could hardly get the
stricken question past her lips.

'I'm such a conniving bastard, I'm afraid,' Luc purred
like a tiger on the prowl.

'You can't want me when I don't want you!' she
gasped.

'I've already disproved that fallacy,' he said drily.
'And, when we reach our destination in England
tomorrow, I have no doubt that you will be in a more
receptive frame of mind.'

All Catherine caught was that one magical word.
'England?' she repeated. 'You're taking me back to
England after the wedding?'

'A change of scene is usual.'

Evidently he believed that, once that ring was on her
finger, it would have the same effect as a chain holding
a skeleton to a dungeon wall. But, once she was back
in England, he couldn't hold her. While she was here,
he had her passport and she wouldn't have liked to bet
on her chances of escape from a walled estate patrolled
by security staff, aided in their task by an impressive
range of electronic devices.

If she didn't go through with the wedding, Drew would
suffer. She shuddered with inner fury at that un-
avoidable conclusion. The seductive fantasy of leaving
Luc without a bride on his much-publicised wedding-
day faded. She should have known better than to think
it could be that easy. All the same, the prospect of being

back in England tomorrow was immensely soothing. He could hardly force her to stay with him.

'Catherine,' Luc drawled. 'Don't even think it.'

'I have nothing to say to you,' she muttered tightly. 'I've already said it all.'

'We have to talk.' A knock sounded on the door. He ignored it. 'I won't allow you to spoil the wedding.'

A gagged and bound bride might raise an eyebrow or two, she reflected fiercely as the knock on the door was repeated.

'Avanti!' Luc called in exasperation.

Bernardo appeared, a secretary just visible behind him. 'Signorina Peruzzi.' He gestured with the cordless phone apologetically. 'She says it is a matter of great urgency that she speak with you, *signor.'*

'I will not take a call from her,' Luc dismissed. 'Leave us, Bernardo.'

The door shut again.

'He speaks English,' Catherine realised. 'Only you must've told him not to around me.'

'The staff are under the illusion that the request was made because you are keen to improve your Italian.'

She covered her face with shaking hands, what composure she had retained threatening all of a sudden to crumble. 'I loathe you!'

'You are angry with me,' he contradicted steadily. 'And I suppose you have some reason for that.'

'You suppose?' Wild-eyed, she surveyed him over the top of her white-boned fingers. Reaction was setting in.

'You belong with me, Catherine. Use the brain God gave you at birth.' The advice was abrasive. 'You have been happy, happier than I have ever known you to be, here.'

'I was living in the past!'

'But why did you choose to return to that particular part of the past?' His sensual mouth twisted. 'Ask yourself that.'

'I didn't choose anything!' she protested. 'And what I ended up with isn't real!'

'It can be as real as you want it to be.'

The sense of betrayal was increasing in her. He had betrayed her. But, worst of all, she had betrayed herself. She had betrayed everything she believed in, everything that she was, everything that she had become after leaving him. In one week she had smashed four years of self-respect. In one week she had destroyed every barrier that might have protected her.

'Can you turn water into wine as well?' she demanded wildly, choking on her own humiliation. 'You must have been laughing yourself sick all week at just how easy it was to make a fool of me!'

A muscle pulled tight at his hard jawline. 'That is not how it has been between us.'

'That's how it's always been between us!' she attacked shakily. 'You plot and you plan and you manipulate and you make things happen just as you want them to happen.'

'I didn't plan for you to lose your memory.'

'But you didn't miss a trick in making use of it!' she condemned. 'And I've been through all this before with you. When we came back from Switzerland, my employers had mysteriously vacated their flat and shut down the art gallery, leaving me out of a job! Coincidence?' she prompted. 'I don't think so. You made that happen as well, didn't you?'

A faint darkening of colour flared over his cheekbones, accentuating the brilliance of his dark eyes. 'I bought the building,' he conceded in a driven tone.

'And it made it so much easier for you to persuade me to come to New York.' Her breath caught like a sob in her throat.

'I wanted you very much. And I was impatient.' He looked at her in unashamed appeal. 'I am what I am, *bella mia*, and I'm afraid I don't have the power to change the past.'

'But I had. Don't you understand that?' Moisture was hitting her eyes in a blinding, burning surge and she could not bear to let him see her cry. 'I had!' she repeated in bitter despair.

'Catherine... what do you want me to say in answer?' he demanded. 'If you want me to be honest, I will be. All that I regret in the past is that I lost you.'

'You didn't lose me... you drove me away!' she sobbed.

He spread eloquent, beautifully shaped hands. 'All right, if semantics are that important, I drove you away. But you might try to see it from my point of view for a change. You shoot a crazy question at me out of the blue one morning over breakfast——'

'Yes, it was crazy, wasn't it?' she cut in tremulously. 'Absolutely crazy of me to think that you might actually condescend to marry me!'

'I didn't know there was going to be no court of appeal!' he slashed back at her fiercely. 'So I said the wrong thing. It was cruel, what I said. I admit that. If you want an apology, you should have stayed around to get it because I don't feel like apologising for it now! I came back to the apartment an hour and a half after I left it that morning. I didn't go to Milan. And where were you?'

She was shattered by the news that he had returned that morning. It shook her right out of her incipient hysteria.

'Yes, where were you?' Luc pressed remorselessly. 'You'd gone. You'd flounced out like a prima donna, leaving everything I'd ever given you, and if you wanted your revenge you got it then in full!'

With a stifled sob, she fled into the bathroom and locked the door, folding down on to the carpet behind it to bury her face in her hands and cry as though her heart was breaking. The past and the present had merged and she could not cope with that knowledge.

CHAPTER SEVEN

WHAT a fool Catherine had been, what a blind, besotted fool! The instant Luc had asked her to marry him, her wits had gone walkabout. So many little things had failed to fit but she had suppressed all knowledge of them, trusting Luc and determined to let nothing detract from her happiness. If it had been his intent to divert her from her amnesia, he could not have been more successful.

How dared he suggest that she had somehow chosen to return to a period of the past when they had still been together? That night in Drew's apartment, Luc had trapped her between two impossible choices. Either she sacrificed Drew or Daniel. With every fibre of her being she would have fought to keep Daniel from Luc.

But Drew also had a strong hold on her loyalty, both in his own right and in his sister's right as well. She owed Harriet a debt she could never repay for helping her when she had hit rock-bottom. How could she have chosen between Daniel and Drew? Faced with the final prospect of telling Luc that he had a son, she had shut her mind down on Daniel to protect him.

Luc poisoned all that he touched. And if he was prepared to marry her simply to ensure her continuing presence in his bed, why shouldn't he accept Daniel as well? Luc, she sensed fearfully, would want his son. Five years ago, Daniel would have been a badly timed, unwelcome complication. Luc had not over-valued her precise importance to him. She was convinced that he would have expected her to have an abortion. But times had changed...

Daniel was innocent and vulnerable, a little boy with a lion-sized intellect often too big for him to handle. Once Luc had been a little boy like that . . . and look how he had turned out. Hard as diamonds. Cold, calculating and callous. Did she want to risk that happening to Daniel? Daniel already had too many of Luc's traits. They had been doled out to him in his genes at birth.

He was strong-willed, single-minded and, if left to his own devices unchecked, exceedingly self-centred. Catherine had spent four and a half years endeavouring to ensure that Daniel grew up as a well-rounded, normal child rather than a remote, hot-house-educated little statistician, divorced by his mental superiority from childish things.

She hated Luc, oh, God, how she hated him! Enshrouded in lonely isolation, she clung ferociously to the hatred that was her only strength. She squashed the sneaking suspicion that Luc was not as callous and cold as she had once believed he was, tuned out the little voice that weakly dared to hint that Luc might have changed. Anger and self-loathing warred for precedence inside her as she cried.

So what if she had to go through the wedding first? As soon as they landed in London, she would leave him. She had done it before; she would to it again, and this time she wouldn't be so dumb. She would take her jewellery with her and sell it. With the aid of that money, she could make a new life for herself and Daniel. She would do it for Daniel's sake.

Misery crept over her with blanket efficiency. It hadn't been real; none of it had been real. She had been living out a fantasy. The background had been so cruelly perfect. A castle for the little girl who had once dreamt about being a princess. A white wedding for the teenager who had once believed in living happily ever after. But, for the woman she was now, there was nothing, less than nothing. And wasn't that her own fault? A grown woman ought to have been able to tell the difference between fantasy and reality.

A certain *je ne sais quoi*, he had called it. A certain three-letter word would have been less impressive but more accurate. Sex. Luc's fatal flaw and probably his only weakness. A certain *je ne sais quoi*, unsought and on many occasions since unwelcome, he had admitted. And you really couldn't blame him for feeling like that, could you? It must be galling to acquire that much wealth and power and discover that you still lusted after a very ordinary little blonde with none of the attributes necessary to embellish your image.

'Catherine? Are you OK?' Luc demanded, startling her.

'You b-bloody snob!' she flared on the back of another sob.

Silence stretched.

'What the hell are you talking about?' he blazed from the other side of the door. 'If you don't come out of there, I'll smash the lock!'

'Force is your answer to everything, isn't it?' Abruptly galvanised into action by the mortifying awareness that he had been listening to her crying, she stood up, stripped off, and walked into the shower, hoping the sound of it would make him go away.

Sex, she thought, loathing him. The lowest possible common denominator. And, after a five-year drought, her value had mushroomed. In fact it had smashed all known stock-market records. In return for unlimited sex, Luc was graciously ready to lower his high standards and marry her. Well, bully for him, and wasn't she a lucky girl?

Little wonder he didn't understand what all the fuss was about. He was sensationally attractive, super-rich and oversexed. Nine out of ten women would contrive

to live with his flaws. Unfortunate that she was the tenth.
Unfortunate for him, that was!

He might get a bride, but he wasn't getting a wife. He
would live to regret forcing her to go through with the
wedding. When she took off within hours of it, the public
embarrassment would be colossal. Then she could stamp
the long-overdue account 'paid in full'. Getting mad got
her nowhere; getting even would restore her self-respect.
Luc might have set her up, but he had set himself up as
well.

Pay-back time was here. She would go down in history
as the woman of principle who had rejected one of the
world's most eligible bachelors. It was perfect, she decided, the old adrenalin flowing again. Shame she
wouldn't be able to stay around to take advantage of
the publicity. She could see the headlines. Why I couldn't
live with Luc Santini.

Tying a towelling robe round her, she abandoned the
entrancing imagery with regret and padded back to the
bedroom, a woman with a mission now, a woman set
on revenge and nobody's victim.

A cork exploded from a bottle like a pistol shot. His
dark head thrown back as he let the excess champagne
foam down into his mouth, Luc was a blaze of stunning
black and gold animal vibrancy in the strong sunlight.
He straightened and poured the mellow golden liquid
expertly into a pair of glasses, white teeth flashing against
brown skin as a brilliant smile curved his mouth. 'Force
is not my answer to everything.' Magnificent lion-gold
eyes skimmed over her. 'You look like a lobster. You've
been in there so long, you must have used up all the hot
water in the castle.'

She hadn't expected him to still be waiting for her.
The filthy look she gave him ought to have withered him.
Naturally it didn't. It drifted impotently off him like a

feather trying to beat up a rock. Crossing the carpet with feline grace, he pressed a glass into her hand. 'You're not in love with Huntingdon,' he drawled. 'If you were, you would have slept with him.'

Just looking at him drained her. Her nerves were suddenly in shreds again. Her hands weren't steady. It was an unequal contest. She wasn't ready for another confrontation and he knew it, conniving and ruthless swine that he was! She marvelled at his arrogance in believing that he could bring her back to heel within the next twenty-four hours. That was, of course, what he was banking on.

'You wouldn't understand a man like Drew if you lived to be a thousand.' Her cheeks had gone all hot, and she tossed back the champagne in the hope of cooling down her temperature.

'He attracts you because he's a loser. You feel sorry for him.'

Her teeth gritted. 'Drew is not a loser.'

'He's run a healthy family firm off its feet with a series of bad business decisions,' Luc traded succinctly.

'And any day of the week, he's still a finer man than you'll ever be!' she launched shakily.

The superb bone-structure hardened. 'You're in a privileged position, *cara*. I would allow no one else to say that to me with impunity.'

The chill she had invoked was intimidating. A shiver ran down her backbone. She felt like a reckless child rebuked for embarrassing the adults. But his contempt for Drew deeply angered her. Yet, at heart, she knew he was right. Drew had never been ambitious or hungry enough to become successful. He had allowed his family to live at a level beyond their means, draining the firm of capital that should have been reinvested for the future. However, those facts didn't lower Drew in her estimation. He was not a born wheeler-dealer and he never would be. When she thought of the dreadful week of worry Drew had had to endure waiting for that contract, she tasted the full threat of Luc's savagery. No...no, she reflected tautly, she would never have cause to regret concealing Daniel's existence from Luc.

'You've hurt Drew,' she whispered, thinking that, once she was gone, Drew would be safe from all interference. She saw no reason to disabuse Luc of his conviction that she had had a relationship with Drew. It infuriated her that Luc should believe he had the right to stare at her with such chilling censure. 'And you don't own me.'

Confusingly, his wide mouth curled into a sudden, almost tender smile. 'I don't need to own you. You are mine, body and soul. So, you strayed a little, got lost, but you didn't stray as far as I'd feared, and now you are back where you belong.'

Seething temper gripped her. 'I don't belong with you!'

'Why do you fight me?' he demanded softly. 'Why do you fight yourself?'

As she collided unwarily with ebony-fringed dark eyes, a squirming helpless sensation kicked at her stomach. It was hard to withstand that burning, blatant self-assurance of his. 'I'm not fighting myself.'

'Come here,' he invited very quietly. 'And prove it.'

The magnetic force of his will was concentrated on her. Her body shivered, though she was not cold, her heart raced, though she was not exerting herself, in re-action to the sheer physical pull he could exert. It crossed her mind crazily that he ought to be banned like a dangerous substance.

He strolled closer and refilled her glass in the throbbing silence. 'You're afraid to,' he noted. 'Indeed, you behave as though you are afraid of me. I don't like that. I don't want a little white ghost with fear in her eyes in my bed tomorrow night. I want that scatty, loving, happy creature you've been all week.'

He was so close now she couldn't breathe. 'I don't love you.'

'If I weren't so certain that you loved me, I wouldn't be marrying you.'

She backed off hastily from his proximity. 'I wouldn't have thought it would have mattered a damn to you either way!'

'If you take refuge in the bathroom again, I'll break the door down,' he delivered conversationally. 'You started this and I'll finish it. I want to know why you're putting up barriers again.'

'Why?' she echoed breathlessly. 'Why? After what you've done?'

A brown hand inscribed a graceful arc. 'What have I done? I spend all these years looking for you and, the moment I find you again, I ask you to marry me. Isn't that a compliment?'

'A c-compliment?'

'It is certainly not an insult, *bella mia*.'

'But I don't want to marry you!'

'I'm becoming fascinated by what must go on in your subconscious mind,' he confessed huskily.

God, he was incredibly attractive. He could talk his way round a lynch mob, she conceded in panic. What she was experiencing right now came down to hormones. That was all. Luc was turning up the heat, stalking her like the pure-bred predator he was. If she lost her head for a second, she would be flat on her back on that bed. Somehow he contrived to say the most outrageous things charmingly. Or maybe it was just that her brain had packed up in disgust at her own frailty.

'You can't persuade me differently with sex either!' she asserted, her spine meeting unexpectedly with a wall that concluded her retreat.

Dancing golden eyes, alight with mockery, arrowed over her. He took her glass from her hand and set it aside. 'We don't have sex, we have intensely erotic experiences,' he countered, his wine-dark voice savouring the syllables.

'Sex!' She hurled the reiteration like a forcefield behind which she might hide. 'And I'm not some tramp... Are you listening to me?'

'I might listen if you say something I want to hear, but you've been rather remiss in that department this afternoon.' Instead of moving closer, he stayed where he was, confusing her. 'And I'm not about to make it easy for you by persuading you into bed.'

She straightened from the wall jerkily, no longer under threat, pink flying into her cheeks. 'You couldn't persuade me.'

'I wouldn't try. I'm saving you up for an intensely erotic experience tomorrow night,' he murmured softly, before closing the door behind him.

She darted after him and turned the key. Then she slumped. Heavens, he was so modest, such a shrinking violet. Wiping her damp forehead, she lay down on the bed, acknowledging, now that he was gone, just how much the past hours of stormy emotion had taken out of her. She had time for a nap before dinner.

She was terribly hot and sticky and thirsty when she woke up. Filling a glass to the brim with flat champagne, she drank it down much as she would have treated lemonade. Had someone been banging on the door a while ago, or was that her imagination?

Nobody's victim, eh? Her earlier fighting thoughts came back to haunt her. Luc had walked the last round. He had switched back to the intimate playful mood of the last few days and she hadn't expected that; she hadn't been prepared. He was in for a heck of a shock when she took her leave at the airport. He hadn't given serious consideration to a single thing she said. Her temper sparked again.

It maddened her to have to admit it, but hating Luc did not make her immune to his physical attraction. It was a hangover from the bad old days—what else could it be? Once she had believed he was a bit like the measles. If you caught him once, you couldn't catch him again.

Evidently the chemistry didn't work like that. Here she was, in full possession of her senses, no longer the doormat *doppelgänger* of recent days, and still she was vulnerable. It enraged her. When he had taken that glass from her and she had thought...she had been in the act of melting down the wall in anticipation.

Pacing about the room in a temper, she helped herself to more champagne. When she had loved Luc, she had just about been able to live with the effect he had on her. When she didn't even like him, never mind love him, it was inexcusable. And as for him—what he deserved was a cheap little tramp, the sort of female prepared to barter sexual favours for his bank balance, the sort of female he ought to understand. That was exactly what he deserved...

She was rifling the dressing-room when the banging on the door interrupted her. Opening it a crack, she found Guilia, for some reason backed by Bernardo, who was holding a large bunch of keys. Her maid looked all hot and flushed and anxious.

'I won't be needing any help tonight. *Grazie*, Guilia.'

'But *signorina*——'

'Dinner will be served in one half-hour,' Bernardo said with a look of appeal.

'I'm sorry, but dinner will have to wait.' Catherine shut the door again. Didn't they all speak great English? When she recalled the sign language she had been reduced to using several times during the week, she cursed Luc. Why had Bernardo looked so shattered at the idea of dinner's having to be held back?

Luc would probably create. Well, so what? It would do him no harm to cool his heels for once. He would appreciate her appearance all the more when she did wander in. Dinner, she decided fiercely, would be fun…fun…fun! However, lest the staff receive the blame for her tardiness, she would be as quick as she possibly could be.

The shimmering tunic top of a black evening suit was extracted from the wardrobe first. It would just cover her hips and, if she wore it back to front, the neckline would be equally abbreviated. Sheer black stockings, no problem. She had every colour of the rainbow. A very high pair of black court shoes were withdrawn next and finally a pair of long black gloves.

Dressed, she walked a slightly unsteady line into the bathroom to go to town on her face. Sapphire and violet outlined her eyes dramatically. Putting on loads of blue mascara, she dabbed gold glitter on her cleavage and traced her lips with strawberry pink. She was starting to enjoy herself. Having moussed her hair into a wild, messy tangle, she went through her jewellery.

She had three diamond bracelets. One went on an ankle, the other two on her wrists over the gloves. A necklace and earrings completed the look. Sort of Christmassy. It was astonishing how cheap diamonds could look when worn to excess. And her wardrobe, shorn of Guilia, had far more adventurous possibilities than Luc could ever have dreamt. The reflection that greeted her in the mirror was satisfyingly startling.

She picked a careful passage down the staircase, aware that she had been a little free with the champagne. Bernardo literally couldn't take his eyes from her as she crossed the hall. He froze, stared, tugged at his tie.

'Evening, Bernardo,' she carolled on her way past. 'It's a hot night, isn't it?'

And it's about to get hotter, she forecast with inner certainty. Abruptly, Bernardo flashed in front of her, spreading wide both doors of the salon. 'Signorina Parrish.'

Why on earth was he announcing her? Did he think Luc wouldn't recognise her under all this gloop? Have her thrown out as a gatecrasher? Taking a deep breath, she launched herself over the threshold. A whole cluster of faces looked back at her, some standing, some sitting. Horror-stricken, she blinked, stage fright taking over. The outfit had been for private viewing only. Behind her, Bernardo was subduing a fit of coughing.

Now that she came to think of it—and thinking was exceedingly difficult at that moment—Luc had mentioned something casual about some close friends coming to stay the night before the wedding. The minute she had shown her nerves at the prospect, he had dropped the subject. Right now, he was undoubtedly wishing he hadn't. Right now, he was remembering that she had a head like a sieve. Right now, as his long lean stride carried him towards her, his eyes were telling her that he wanted to kill her, inch by painful inch, preferably over a lengthy period. And that he intended to enjoy every minute of it when he got the chance.

'Say, I thought it was fancy dress,' she muttered and attempted to sidle out again, but Luc snaked out a hand and cut off her escape.

'She's so avant-garde,' a youthful female voice gasped. 'Mummy, why can't I wear stuff like that?'

'Designer punk,' someone else commented. 'Very arresting.'

'And I wouldn't mind being arrested with her.' A tall, very good-looking blond man sent her a sizzling smile. 'Luc, I begin to understand why you kept this charming lady under wraps until the very last moment. I'm Christian... Christian Denning.'

Catherine shook his hand with a smile. He had bridged an awkward silence. A whirl of introductions took place. There were about thirty people present, an even mix of nationalities, fairly split between the business élite and the upper crust. It was a relief when she finally made it into a seat to catch her breath.

'You have the most fabulous legs.' Christian dropped down on to the arm of her sofa. 'Why do I have the feeling that Luc would rather have kept the view an exclusive one?'

'Have you known Luc for long?' she asked in desperation.

'About ten years. And I saw you at a distance once in Switzerland, seven years ago,' he confided in an undertone. 'That was as close as I was allowed to get.'

A wave of heat consumed her skin. This was someone who had to have a very fair idea of what her former association with Luc had been. 'Was it?' She tried to sound casual.

'Luc's very possessive,' he responded mockingly. 'But he must have snatched you right out of your cradle. I must remember to tease him about that.'

Luc strolled over. 'Enjoying yourself, Christian?'

'Immensely. There isn't a man in the room who doesn't envy me. Why did I have to wait this long to meet her?'

'Perhaps I foresaw your reaction.' Luc reached for Catherine's hand. It was time to go into dinner. 'Everybody likes you,' he breathed, pressing his mouth with fleeting brevity to her bare shoulder, fingertips skating caressingly down her taut spinal cord. 'You forgot they were coming, didn't you?' He was smiling at her, she registered dazedly. '*Cara*, if you had seen your face when you realised what you had done! But in this gathering you don't look quite as shocking as you no doubt thought you would.'

On that point, he was correct. There was no conventional garb on display. At this level, the women were more interested in looking different from each other. She might look startling to her own eyes and to those of anyone who knew her, but nobody was likely to suspect that she had deliberately dressed up as some sort of pantomime hooker. Had it been her intent to embarrass Luc in company, she would not have succeeded and, since that had not been her intent, she was relieved until it occurred to her that he would endure more than embarrassment when she walked out on him at the airport. A sneaking twinge of guilt assailed her. Immediately she was furious with herself. Luc had set the rules and she was playing by *his* rules now. He had given her no other choice. What transpired, therefore, was of his own making.

A middle-aged woman with a beaky nose took a seat to the left of her at the dining-table and asked, 'Do you hunt?'

'Only when I lose something,' Catherine replied abstractedly.

Someone hooted with amusement as though she had said something incredibly witty. A wry smile curved Luc's mouth. 'Catherine's not into blood sports.'

'She must be planning to reform you, then,' a blonde in cerise silk said with smiling sarcasm. 'Blood sports are definitely your forte.'

'And yours, sister, dear,' Christian interposed drily.

The long meal was not the ordeal she had expected but it was impossible for her to relax. Luc was in an exceptionally good mood, which somehow had made her feel uncomfortable. She was flagging by the time the Viennese coffee was served in the *salone*. Christian's sister settled down beside her and she struggled to recall her name. Georgina, that was it.

'I didn't see you with Luc in Nice last week,' Georgina remarked.

'I wasn't there.'

Georgina contrived to look astonished. 'But he was with Silvana Lenzi. Naturally, I assumed... Oh, dear, have I said something I oughtn't?'

'You've said exactly what you intended to say, young lady,' the kindly woman with the beaky nose retorted crisply, and changed the subject.

Across the room, Luc was laughing with a group of men. Catching her eye, he gave her a brilliant smile. Hurriedly, she glanced away. Her nails dug into the soft flesh of her palm. She really couldn't understand why she should feel so shattered. Luc had not spent the past four and a half years without a woman in his bed. Celibacy would come no more naturally to him than losing money.

The South American film actress was notorious for her passionate affairs. He certainly hadn't been boldly going where no man had gone before, Catherine thought with a malice that shook her. She was speared by a Technicolor picture of that beautiful, lean, muscular, suntanned body of his engaged in intimate love-play with the gorgeous redhead. It made her feel sick. She felt betrayed.

Obviously she had had too much to drink. It had unsettled her stomach, confused her thoughts. If she felt betrayed, it was only because she had been the chosen one this week and the awareness was bound to distress her. Really, she didn't care if he had been throwing orgies in Nice. His womanising habits were a matter of the most supreme indifference to her.

A few minutes later, Luc interceded to conclude her evening. She was tired. He was sure everyone would excuse her. With his usual panache, he swept her out of the *salone*. She shook off his arm with distaste.

'It's ten minutes to midnight.' Impervious to hints, he was reaching for her. 'Isn't it supposed to be bad luck for me to see you after midnight?' he teased, glittering golden eyes tracking over her in the most offensively proprietorial way.

Without even thinking about it, Catherine lifted her arm and slapped him so hard across one cheekbone that she almost fell. 'That's for Nice!' she hissed, stalking up the staircase. 'And if I see you after midnight, it won't be just bad luck, it'll be a death-trap!'

'Buona notte, carissima,' he said softly, almost amusedly.

Incredulous at the response, she halted and turned her head.

He stared up at her and smiled. 'You're crazy, but I like it.'

'What's the matter with you?' she snapped helplessly.

He checked his watch. 'You have six minutes to make it out of my sight. If you start talking, you'll never make it.'

Her fingermarks were clearly etched on one high cheekbone. The sight of her own handiwork filled her with sudden shame. She really didn't know what had come over her. 'I'm sorry. I shouldn't have done that,' she conceded.

'I'd forgive you for anything tonight. Even keeping me awake,' he advanced huskily.

That did it. She raced up to her room as though all the hounds in hell were pursuing her.

The beautiful breakfast brought to Catherine on a tray couldn't tempt her. The hair-stylist arrived, complete with retinue, followed by the cosmetics consultant and then the manicurist. The constant female chatter distanced her from the proceedings. As the morning moved on, she felt more and more as if she were a doll playing

a part. She had nothing to do. Everyone else did it for
her. And finally they stood back, hands were clapped,
mutually satisfied smiles exchanged and compliments
paid . . . the doll was dressed.

It wasn't real, not really real, she told herself repeatedly and stole another glance at her reflection, for
it so closely matched that teenage dream. Certainly she
had never before looked this good. No wonder they were
all so pleased with themselves.

The little church was only a mile from the castle. It
had been small and plain and dark when she had seen
it earlier in the week. Today it was ablaze with flowers
that scented the air heavily. She was in a daze. She went
down the short aisle on the arm of a Spanish duke she
had only met the night before. It's five years too late,
five years too late; this doesn't mean anything to me
now, she reasoned at a more frantic pitch as Luc swung
round to take a long unashamed look at her. But
somehow from that moment she found it quite impossible to reason at all.

'The most beautiful bride I've ever seen.' Luc brushed
his lips very gently across hers and the combination of
a rare compliment and physical contact sent her senses
reeling dizzily.

Sunlight was warming her face, glinting off the twist
of platinum on her finger next, and Christian was
dropping a kiss on her brow, laughingly assuring her
that Luc had said her mouth was out of bounds.

In the limousine, he caught her to him and took her
mouth with all the hunger he had earlier restrained. Her
bouquet dropped from her fingers, fell forgotten to the
floor, and her arms went round his neck, her unsteady
fingers linking in an unbroken chain to hold him to her.

CHAPTER EIGHT

VIOLINS were thrumming in Catherine's bloodstream. She drifted round the floor in a rosy haze of contentment.

'Catherine?'

'Hmm?' she sighed dreamily into Luc's shoulder, opening her eyes a chink and vaguely surprised to recognise that the light, cast by the great chandeliers above, was artificial. In her mind she had been waltzing out under the night stars. 'Candles would have been more atmospheric,' she whispered, and then, 'You're thinking of the fire hazard and the smoke they would have created.'

'I'm trying very hard not to. I know what's expected of me,' Luc confessed above her head, and she gave a drowsy giggle. A lean hand tipped her face back, lingered to cup her chin. 'It's time for us to leave.'

'L-leave?' she echoed, jolted by the announcement.

His thumb gently eased between her parted lips and rimmed the inviting fullness of the lower in a gesture that was soul-shatteringly sensual. A heady combination of drowning feminine weakness and excitement spread burning heat through her tautening muscles. He might as well have thrown a high-voltage switch inside her. Dark eyes shaded by ebony lashes glimmered with gold. 'Leave,' he repeated, the syllables running together and merging. 'Fast,' he added as an afterthought.

'Everybody's still here.' She trembled as the hand resting at her spine curved her into contact with the stirring hardness of his thighs. 'Oh.'

'As you say, *cara*...oh,' he murmured softly. 'Our guests will dance quite happily to dawn without me. I have other ambitions.'

Her body was dissolving in the hard circle of his arms. She would have gone anywhere, done anything to stay there. The very thought of detaching herself long enough to get changed scared her. She was waking up out of the dream-like haze which had floated her through the day. And waking up was absolutely terrifying.

Had she really been stubborn enough to cling to the conviction that she hated him? It hadn't been hatred she'd felt when she saw him at the altar. It wasn't hatred she felt when he touched her. It was love. Love. She was blitzed by that reality. Her emotions had withstood the tests of pain and disillusionment, time and maturity. Why? But she knew why; scarcely had to answer the question. And in the beginning there was Luc...and there ended her story.

He steered her out of the ballroom, quite indifferent to the conversational sallies of several cliques in their path. In the shadow of the great staircase, he moulded her against him, his mouth hard and urgent, long fingers framing her cheekbones as he kissed her, at first roughly, then lingeringly with a slow, drugging sexuality that devastated her.

A low-pitched wolf-whistle parted them. Hot-cheeked, still trembling with the force of the hunger Luc had summoned up, she let her hands slide down from his shoulders, steadying herself.

Christian was regarding them from several feet away, a smile of unconcealed amusement on his face. Dealing him an unembarrassed glance, Luc directed her upstairs with the thoughtful precision of someone who doubted her ability to make it there without assistance. Guilia was waiting to help her out of her gown.

Dear God, Catherine thought in numbed confusion, was there a strong streak of insanity in her bloodline? Nothing less than madness could excuse her behaviour over the past twenty-four hours. Did all women lie to themselves as thoroughly as she had? Luc knew her better than she knew herself. He knew her strengths and insecurities, her likes and dislikes, even, it seemed, her craven habit of avoiding what she couldn't handle and denying what she was afraid of...

Why did she deceive herself this way? She had been like a child with an elaborate escape-plan, a child who secretly wanted to be caught before she did any real damage. Almost seven years ago she had given her heart without the slightest encouragement, and that heart was still his. And that love was something she couldn't change, something that was simply a part of her, something that it was quite useless to fight. Luc was her own personal self-destruct button. But leaving him less than five years ago had still been like tearing her heart from her body.

'I need you,' he had said once in the darkness of the night in Switzerland. The admission had turned her over and inside out. She would have walked on fire for him just for those three little words. But he had never said them again, never even come close to saying them once he had been secure in the knowledge that she adored him.

It hadn't been very long before he'd begun to smoothly remind her that what they had wouldn't last forever. He had hurt her terribly. He had taught her to walk floors at night, to feel sick at a careless word or oversight, to panic if a phone call was late... to live from day to day with this dreadful nagging fear of losing him always in the background. Inside, where it didn't show, he had killed her by degrees.

'He was very bad for you,' Harriet had scolded.
'You're not cut out to cope with someone like that. But
you did what you had to do. You protected Daniel. Be
proud that you had that much sense.'

Whenever she had wavered, as waver she had for far
longer than she wanted to recall, Harriet had been the
little Dutch boy, sticking her finger in the dam-wall of
her emotions, preventing the leak from developing into
a torrent that might prompt her into some foolish action.
Oh, yes, she had thought about phoning him times
without number. She had always chickened out. Once
she had even stood in the post office a couple of days
before his birthday, crazy enough to consider sending
him a card because she knew that since his family's death
there was nobody else but her to remember. Harriet had
had her work cut out and no mistake. That first year
keeping her away from Luc had been a full-time
occupation.

But Catherine had been lucky enough to have had
Daniel on whom to target her emotions. How could
anyone understand what Daniel meant to her? The first
time she held him in her arms she had wept incon-
solably. Nobody but Harriet had understood. Daniel had
been the first living person she had ever seen to whom
she was truly related. Between them, Daniel and Harriet
had become the family she had never had.

Why had she planned to leave Luc again? This time
she was honest with herself about her most driving mo-
tivation. She was terrified of telling him about Daniel,
as terrified as she had been when she had realised she
was pregnant. Luc did not have and clearly never had
had the smallest suspicion that she might have been
pregnant.

It was all so horribly complicated and she had so much
to lose. Daniel believed his father was dead. He had
asked very few questions and she really hadn't under-

stood that he actually resented not having a father until that day at Greyfriars when he had raged at her, naïvely sharing his secret belief that his father, had he still been alive, would have been able to work miracles.

Daniel would accept Luc with very little encouragement. How Daniel would react to the discovery that his mother had lied to him was another question entirely. And could she trust Luc with Daniel? Daniel was very insecure right now, very breakable. If Luc could not accept him wholeheartedly, Daniel would know it. In addition, he was illegitimate. That couldn't be hidden and, sooner or later, it would hit the newspapers. Luc would find that intolerable.

And on what basis did she dare to assume that Luc saw their marriage as a permanent fixture? Luc was so unpredictable. Did she turn Daniel's life upside-down in the hope that Luc could come to terms with the decision she had made five years ago, and the fact that he had a four-year-old son?

Yesterday she had believed she had a choice. Today she accepted that she had merely talked herself into taking the easy way out and running away again. It wouldn't work this time. And the irony was that she didn't want it to work anyway. She loved Luc. She wanted to hope. She wanted to trust. She wanted to believe that somehow all this could be worked out. And that meant telling Luc about Daniel.

There was no time to be lost. The day after tomorrow, Peggy would be driving down to London. How did she tell him? The enormity of the announcement she had to make sunk in on her, another razor edge to hone her nerves. She would tell him on the flight to London ... it wouldn't be very private, though. She would tell him whenever they arrived at their destination, wherever that was. But the more she dwelt on the coming confrontation, the more panic-stricken she became at the prospect.

'You're very pale.'

In the limousine, she didn't feel up to that narrowed, probing gaze. How would Luc react? That was all she could think about. Yesterday she had been telling herself that he was cold, callous and calculating in an effort to shore up her reluctance to tell him about Daniel. Yesterday she had been determined to hate him, determined to see him as a threat to Daniel. Now she had come down out of the clouds again, but the view was no more encouraging. She had deceived him. She had lied by omission. Those who crossed Luc lived to regret the miscalculation. Since she had never put herself in that position before, how could she possibly predict how he would react?

'And very quiet,' Luc continued.

She gulped. 'I was just thinking.'

'About what?'

'Nothing in particular.' She veiled her troubled eyes in case he did what he had done before and read her mind. Do it now, do it now, she urged herself. You know what you're like. The longer you leave it, the bigger mess you'll make of it. 'What time do we arrive in London?'

'Didn't I tell you? The air-traffic controllers in Rome are having a twenty-four-hour stoppage,' he imparted with the utmost casualness. 'We fly to London early tomorrow morning.'

'We're not going to the airport?' she gasped.

'A friend has offered us the use of his villa overnight.'

Her hands clenched convulsively together. Reprieve, the coward in her thought. An opportunity to be alone with him and tell him, her conscience insisted. The limousine was already turning through tall gates.

A housekeeper greeted them on the steps. When Luc refused the offer of supper, they were shown upstairs to a bedroom suite. It was full of mirrors and exotic silks and the most enormous bed. This was her wedding night, she reflected in despair. How could she tell him tonight? It would ruin the whole day, she reasoned weakly.

He came up behind her and buried his mouth hotly against the soft, sensitive spot where her shoulder met her throat, and her knees buckled. 'We should have supper,' she managed shakily.

'Are you hungry?'

'Well——'

'Supper wouldn't satisfy my hunger either,' he breathed approvingly. Slowly, heart-stoppingly, he turned her round. 'What's wrong with you?' he enquired, completely without warning.

'W-wrong?'

'You have the look of a murderer caught burying the body,' he murmured thoughtfully. 'Or is that my imagination?'

'Your imagination.' Avoiding his far too perceptive eyes, she tried to sidetrack him by reaching up and starting to undo his tie.

'My imagination rarely plays tricks on me.' He watched her struggling with his tie. With an expressive sigh, he covered her small shaking hands with one of his. 'You don't trust me, do you? I won't hurt you ever again, *bella mia*. I promise you that.'

Unbearably touched and suddenly rent with guilt, her eyes clouded over.

'I was only twenty-seven when I met you.' He ran a questing fingertip along the taut curve of her cheek. 'And I didn't want to meet someone like you. I set out to get you on my terms and I knew it wasn't what you wanted or what you deserved. You loved me too much, *cara*. You let me get away with murder. So, I took you for granted.' His superb bone-structure was prominent beneath his suntanned skin, his eyes very dark. 'I thought you would always be there. And then one day you were gone and I realised that even you had your breaking point. I realised that a little too late for it to make any difference.'

'Luc, I——'

He brushed his fingers in a silencing motion against her lips. 'I don't want to talk about the past now. It casts shadows. Maybe tomorrow, maybe the next day, hmm?' he cajoled. 'But not tonight.'

She turned her mouth involuntarily into the warm palm of his hand, tears wet on her cheeks. He appealed to her for understanding and Luc was not given to appeals. Strain clenched his dark features. The break with the tradition of keeping his own counsel hurt.

He trailed his tie off, shed his jacket with a lithe twist of his shoulders and pulled her into his arms, emanating now all the raw self-assurance that came so naturally to him. 'I scarcely slept last night,' he admitted softly. 'And I intend to keep you awake all night as punishment.'

His breath warmed her cheek and then his tongue slid between her lips, thrusting them apart to explore the moist interior she so freely offered him. The floor under her feet seemed to fall away, and she clung to him while he took her mouth again and again with a stormy intensity that stirred a dulled ache in the pit of her stomach. Her silk dress pooled on the carpet without her even being aware that he was expertly removing it. Lean fingers slid caressingly over her hip, encountering lace, and, disregarding the fragile barrier, he made her jerk and moan beneath his marauding mouth.

He laughed soft and deep in his throat, ceasing the provocation only to pick her up and carry her over to the bed, following her down in fluid motion, reacquainting her with every sleek line of his lean body. His shirt had come adrift and she ran her hands up over his smooth brown back, feeling every muscle tauten to her reconnaissance. He ground his hips sensuously slowly into hers, and for mindless seconds she was ruled by the hunger he could evoke and completely lost.

He looked down at her, dark eyes aflame with gold satisfaction and desire. 'Remember that first night in Switzerland?' he whispered huskily. 'You were so exquisitely shy.' He strung a line of kisses across her delicate collarbone. 'So innocent. I was a bastard, *bella mia*. It should have been our wedding night.'

'I pretended it was.'

A faint flush of colour irradiated the high cheekbones that intensified his raw attraction. He captured the fingers lacing into his black silky hair and pressed them to his lips, dense lashes concealing his gaze. 'I'd never made love to a virgin before. I wanted it to be special for you. That's why I took you to Switzerland.'

'It was special,' she managed unsteadily. 'Very special.'

'*Grazie... grazie tanto, cara,*' he teased. 'It was so special for me that I had to keep you all to myself, being of a naturally selfish disposition.'

She had never seen him so relaxed, not this last week, not ever. But for a split second he reminded her so powerfully of Daniel. The same beautiful dark eyes, the same wide mouth that could yank at her heart-strings with the faintest smile. Her breath caught in her throat, but he was brushing aside the lace cups of her bra, letting his tongue and then his mouth circle the taut pink nipples he had uncovered, and her mind became a complete blank, her fingers clenching together as sensation began to build, drawing every tiny muscle tight beneath his ministrations.

There was a mirror above the bed. She blinked bemusedly and then the imagery of his brown hands on her paler skin and his dark head bent so intimately over her took over. 'There's a mirror up there,' she whispered.

'How shocking.' His voice was indistinct, abstracted. 'Tell Christian he has outrageous bad taste next time you see him.'

'This is his villa?'

Luc eased back from her reluctantly, rolled off the bed and proceeded to strip. She couldn't take her eyes from him. Wide shoulders tapered down to a narrow waist, lean hips and long, muscular thighs. He was very aroused, superbly male, supremely beautiful.

'Looking at me like that does nothing for my self-control.' He came down beside her again, dispensed with the wispy lingerie and curved her into his arms. The dark hair hazing his chest rubbed against her tender breasts, one lean thigh hooking over hers as he stared down at her, so much unashamed hunger in his probing appraisal that she was breathless. 'You wouldn't have done it.'

'Done what?'

'Walked away at the airport.' A wry smile challenged her shock. 'I wouldn't have let you go. Did you think I didn't know? Sometimes I know what you think before you think it.'

Having devastated her, he took advantage by ravishing her swollen mouth with a fierce, driving sweetness. Time and thought were banished. She got drunk on the taste of him. The warm masculine scent of him flooded her, making her even more light-headed. She could feel herself sliding out of control. Breathing hurt her lungs. Tiny sounds she was barely conscious of broke from her lips, and when his hand touched her where she most ached for fulfilment, she went wild, writhing with his burning caresses, hungrily searching out for herself the compulsive heat of his mouth.

It was agony and ecstasy but he wouldn't give her what she sought as she blindly arched her hips in a silent expression of need as old as time. She was twisting in the heat of a fire that demanded assuagement. Her fingernails raked his back in torment and protest. And then, in the shuddering, explosive tension of his body, she felt the flames leap and scorch through him as well. Suddenly he was all aggressor, all savage demand, spreading her out like a sacrifice to some primitive god and falling on her, hands bruising her thighs as he took her with all the strength he possessed in a driving surge of passionate intensity.

It went on and on and on, more and then incredibly more until she was sobbing her pleasure out loud, lost to everything but the remorseless demands of her own body. The release came in a frenzied explosion of exquisite sensation that left her awash with the bliss of satiation.

'*Dio!*' he groaned in harsh satisfaction, shuddering in the possessive circle of her arms, burying his damp face in her hair. '*Te amo,*' he muttered, almost crushing her beneath his weight. '*Te amo.*'

She stilled. I love you. I love you, he had said.

'*Scusi.*' He rolled over and sprawled back in an indolent tangle of sun-darkened limbs against the white percale sheeting. 'Now I finally know what it's like to be a sex object,' he sighed without particular concern in the winging smile he angled at her. 'You made me lose control. That's my department.'

She smiled, a fat-cat-got-the-cream smile. He probably didn't even know he'd said it. That was fine. The last thing she wanted to do was to make an issue out of it. She had lived off 'I need you' for almost two years once. She could manage a good decade on 'I love you'. Moving over, she scattered a trail of kisses across a sweat-slicked broad shoulder. 'I love you . . . I love you . . . I love you,' she whispered feverishly.

He caught a hand into her tousled hair. 'I know, I know, I know,' he said playfully.

He hadn't bitten the bait. When did he? She was too impatient. If he had meant it, he would tell her in his own good time. If? It didn't help to be aware that such a confession at the height of sexual excitement was recorded the world over as a statutory and meaningless phrase. But didn't she have rather more to worry about right now? Daniel rose like Mount Everest in the back of her mind.

'Luc...how do you feel about children?'

He tugged her down on top of him, claimed a kiss, clearly not very focused on the concept of dialogue. 'I never thought of them until recently.'

'Do...do you like them?'

'Like them?' Ebony brows slashed together in a frown. 'What sort of a question is that? I expect I will like my own. I have no real interest in other people's.'

It wasn't very encouraging. She made no demur when his hands started to roam lazily over her again. Indeed, she needed that closeness, that hunger of his to control the fear that was steadily rising inside her. Luc would be furious. But what frightened her most was the unknown quantity of how he would react after the fury.

'You can sleep during the flight.' Luc smiled down into her heavy eyes, satisfaction and amusement mingling in his scrutiny.

They were about to leave the VIP lounge when a small grey-haired man, closely followed by a security guard, came in.

'Antonio?' Luc crossed the room to greet him with pleated brows.

The low-pitched exchange of Italian had an odd edge of urgency that made Catherine glance in their direction. The older man gave something to Luc, withdrew a handkerchief to mop his perspiring brow and, by his manner, was clearly apologising. He looked as though he was reporting a death. She stifled a yawn, and her attention slewed away again.

'Who was that?' she asked as they boarded the jet.

'One of my lawyers.' His intonation was curiously clipped.

She hated take-off; always had. She didn't open her eyes until they were airborne. Luc wasn't beside her. On the other side of the cabin, he was scanning a single sheet of paper. As she watched he scrunched it up between his fingers and snatched up the newspaper lying on the desk in front of him. He signalled to the steward with a snap of his fingers. A large whiskey arrived pronto. Draining it in one long, unappreciative gulp, he suddenly sprang up, issuing a terse instruction to the steward who left the cabin at speed.

'Catherine...come here.' He moved a hand in an oddly constrained arc.

Releasing her belt, she got up. His set profile was dark, brooding. He indicated the seat opposite. 'Sit down.'

When she collided with his eyes her heart stopped beating and her mouth ran dry. The suppressed violence that sprang out at her from that hawk-like stare of intimidation was terrifying.

'I will not lose my head with you,' he asserted in a controlled undertone. 'There must be an explanation. I still have faith, but it hangs by a thread.'

'You're scaring me.'

He continued to study her, a kind of flagellating stare that threatened to strip the skin from her facial bones. 'Last week, Rafaella told me something I refused to believe. After your disappearance five years ago, she stayed in the apartment we shared for some weeks. I didn't want it to be empty if you phoned or chose to return.'

Uncertainly she nodded.

'And last week she informed me that during her stay a call came from some doctor's surgery, asking why you hadn't been back for a check-up.'

She bent her head and studied the desk-top, goose-flesh prickling at the nape of her neck, an impending sense of doom sliding over her.

'From that call and certain trivia she subsequently un-covered in the apartment,' Luc continued in the same murderously calm tone, 'Rafaella deduced that you were pregnant at the time of your departure.'

She flinched, froze, watched the desk-top blur.

'She assumed—that is, if her story is true—that you had decided on an abortion. She told me that at the time she saw no good reason to share this knowledge with me. So she cultivated a short memory.'

Catherine wanted God to pluck her out of the sky and put her somewhere out of Luc's reach. Her vocal cords were in arrest. Her brain had stopped functioning.

'Naturally her assumption was that, if there was a child, it was not mine. Halston figured largely as the culprit,' he extended, his tone quieter and quieter, every word slow and precise and measured. 'Perhaps you can now understand why I was so angry with her. After this length of time the story struck me as fantastic and wholly incredible. I didn't believe a word of it. I defended you.'

The weight of the world's sins seemed to sit on her bowed shoulders. She was shrinking inwardly and outwardly.

'This is now your cue to tell me that not a word of her story is true. You see, Rafaella is persistent. When I refused her calls, she communicated with one of my lawyers in Rome, giving him the details of what she ap-parently discovered in England,' he spelt out. 'Antonio spent a most troubled night before rousing the courage to bring those facts to me. He was hastened to a decision when an article purporting to relate to you was printed in an English newspaper.'

'I...I didn't think of it coming out like this!' she burst out strickenly. 'I intended to tell you when we arrived in England...' Her voice trailed away.

'Look at me.' He ground out the command fiercely. 'Are you telling me it is true? That you were pregnant? That there is a child?'

Like a puppet she nodded twice, shorn of speech by the violent incredulity splintering from him in waves.

'And...you...married...me?' He was rising slowly from behind the desk, having trouble in getting the question past his compressed lips.

'What did you expect me to do?' she muttered frantically.

'What did I expect? What did I expect?' he roared at her, a hand like a vice closing round her wrist to trail her bodily out of her seat.

'You're hurting me!'

'He'd better not be mine!' he bit down at her rawly.

The tension broke her and she sobbed, 'Of course he is. Of course he's yours. Why would you want anything else?'

He punched a fist into the palm of his other hand with a sickening thud and swung violently away from her. Barbaric fury throbbed from every tensed line of his long, taut body. 'If I touch you, I'll kill you. *Cristo*, get out of my sight before I lose control!'

'Luc, please,' she said brokenly.

He spun back to her, fluid as a cat on his feet even in rage. 'If he hadn't been mine, maybe...just maybe I could have forgiven you, because then at least I could have understood why you ran away. But this!' He spread brown hands eloquently wide in a slashing movement. 'This I don't understand at all!'

'If you would just calm down,' she interposed pleadingly.

'Calm down? I find out I have a son of almost five whom I don't know and I never even dreamt existed, and you ask me to calm down?'

'I should have told you last night.'

'Last night?' he grated in disbelief. 'Last night, while you were playing the whore in my arms, I'd definitely have strangled you! I don't give a damn about last night or last week! I'm talking about five years ago when you were pregnant!'

The brutality of his attack on her behaviour the night before cut with the efficacy of a knife through her heart. 'S-stop shouting——'

'If I don't shout I'll get physical! And I've never struck a woman in my life and I will not start now,' he shot at her furiously.

It took immense will-power for her to drag her thoughts into order. The sheer force of his rage had shattered her, and his contention that he would have preferred to learn that Daniel was another man's child was quite incomprehensible to her.

'Why didn't you tell me five years ago?' The repetition scorched back at her.

'I meant to...I tried to——'

'I don't remember you trying,' he cut in ruthlessly.

She sucked in air convulsively. 'I was afraid to tell you.'

He uttered a succinct swear-word he had never used in her presence before. It blazed with his derision.

'All right,' she whispered, and, mustering the tattered shreds of her composure, she mastered herself sufficiently to continue. 'You won't like what I'm about to say...'

'I don't like you,' he breathed with chilling effect. 'Nothing that you could say could be any worse than the revulsion I feel now.'

Unintentionally she burst into tears, hating herself for the weakness, but she felt as if she were an animal caught in a trap.

'I couldn't bring myself to tell you,' she formulated shakily, 'because I knew you wouldn't want him and I was scared that I would let you talk me into getting rid of him.'

'You dare to foist the blame on me!' he raked back at her with contempt.

In a benumbed state, she moved her head back and forth. 'You always made it so obvious that you didn't want to commit yourself to me in any way. I honestly believed that you would see a termination as the only practical solution.'

'Where my own flesh and blood is concerned, I am not practical! And what does commitment to you have to do with commitment to my unborn child?' he demanded. 'And what do you know of my feelings about abortion? When did we ever discuss the subject?'

'I . . . I made an assumption,' she conceded, no longer able to look at him.

'You made one hell of an assumption!'

'At the time, I believed it was the right one,' she whispered.

'And shall I tell you why you made that assumption? Look at me!' he commanded fiercely, and she did, fearfully, sickly, wondering where the axe could possibly fall next. 'I never knew what a temper you had. I never dreamt there could be such bitterness and obstinacy behind that angel face. But I know it now, and I don't need your interpretation, for I have my own! Let me tell you how it was: if I wasn't going to marry you, I would pay for that with the loss of my child!'

'No!' she cried. 'It wasn't like that!'

'It was exactly like that. No ring, no child. I was playing Russian roulette over that breakfast table and I didn't know it!' He looked at her with hatred. 'To think that I tortured myself over what I said to you that day! You had no right to conceal the truth from me. It was my right to know that you were carrying my child. *Cristo*, did you hate me so much that you couldn't even give me a chance?'

Her legs were shaking. She sank down in the nearest seat and covered her face with damp hands. 'I loved you. I loved you so much.'

'*That* was love?' He emitted a harsh laugh of incredulity. 'I lash out at you once. In nearly two years, I lose my temper with you once! Once! And I've been paying for it ever since. It was revenge you took, and I understand revenge very well.'

'I don't think like you,' she said in defeat.

'If you thought like me, you'd have been my wife five years ago! *Si*, I'd have married you.' Lancing dark eyes absorbed her white face with a kind of grim satisfaction. 'I probably wouldn't have done it with the best of grace, but I'd have married you.'

She shrank in retrospect from such a fate. Luc, forced into marriage shotgun-style. It would have been a nightmare. 'I wouldn't have wanted you to marry me feeling like that.'

'*Dio!* What would your feelings or my feelings have had to do with it with a child on the way?'

'I couldn't have lived with you under those circumstances,' she muttered limply.

His mouth twisted chillingly. 'The only truly honest woman I ever met—that's what I told Rafaella about you. It's a wonder she didn't laugh in my face! But then, she has one virtue you don't have. She's loyal even when I turn on her as I did last week.'

'Daniel and I will go away.' Hardly knowing what she was saying, Catherine spoke the thought out loud. 'You won't hear from us again.'

CHAPTER NINE

'YOU'RE not taking him anywhere!'

'You don't want him. You didn't even want him to be yours. That has to be the sickest, cruellest thing you've ever said to me.' Catherine's voice wobbled alarmingly on the contention.

'Sick?' Luc thundered. 'I've lost five years of his life! He's illegitimate. What will he suffer in later years? Don't you realise that all this will hit the papers? Did you think you'd be able to shelter behind the fallacy that you were a widow with a child for the rest of your days? It will come out...of course it will, and how will the child feel then? About you? About me? That is why my first wish was that he should not be mine. For *his* sake, not my own. The papers are already sifting what few facts they have, already hinting that all is not as it appears. Why else was he left in England?'

'The papers?' She was ghost-pale, paralysed by the sheer force of the condemnation coming her way.

'Surely you didn't believe that you could step from nowhere into the life that I lead and conceal the truth? If it hadn't been for Rafaella, his face would already have been splashed all over the gutter Press! When she tracked him down to your friend's home in the Lake District, she got him out before the paparazzi could make a killing.'

'Got him out? To take him where?' she pressed feverishly, registering that the threat of Press interest had been roused far more swiftly than she had naïvely expected.

160

'She persuaded your friend to bring him south before the Press arrived. They're waiting for us at the house.'

'What house?' she mumbled dazedly.

His strong jawline clenched, a tiny muscle tugging at the hardened line of his mouth. 'I bought it for you as a wedding present. Five years ago... five long, wasted years ago!' he vented rawly.

In the state she was in, it took a little while for the significance of that admission to sink in. 'Five years ago?'

Smouldering dark eyes black as pitch bit into her. 'I was such a fool. I, who prided myself on my superior judgement! Haven't you worked it out yet, *cara*? I was in love with you.'

'F-five years ago?' It was a shattered gasp.

'I didn't know it myself until you had gone.' His inflexion, his whole demeanour, was chillingly cold and harsh. 'The last laugh really was on me. I believed you would return... phone... send a postcard with "x marks the spot" on it... something, anything! I couldn't believe you would stay away forever. I could not have done that to you.' That confession appeared to awaken another scorching tide of anger. His teeth gritted as he stared at her. 'I spent a fortune trying to trace you. In an excess of conscience-stricken self-reproach, I intended to marry you as soon as I found you! So much for the fresh start!'

Slow tears brimmed up in her eyes and rolled down her cheeks. She swallowed back her sobs in the seething silence that throbbed and tortured and taunted. But Luc was not finished with her.

'And when I find you, I close my eyes to the evidence of what you are. I make excuses for you. I cling to an illusion that probably never existed anywhere outside my own imagination. Why?' A savage bitterness stamped his dark taut features. 'It can only be because you're the best lay I've ever had. That is all I will ever allow it to be now.'

'Don't,' she begged brokenly, sensing his destructive determination to smash the bonds between them...or had she already done that for herself?

'You did this to me before. I will never let you do it to me again.' The assurance carried all the lethal conviction of an oath.

'What did I do?' she whispered.

'Five years ago I trusted you more than anyone else in this world, Catherine. And you betrayed that trust,' he delivered contemptuously. 'You spent all night in my arms, telling me how much you loved me and then you walked out...'

'I was saying goodbye the only way I could.' It was a dulled murmur.

'Of course, it would not occur to you that one of the reasons I was so angry with you the next morning was that I felt that I had been set up!'

'How could you feel that?'

'How could I fail to feel that? And then I didn't want to marry you, I didn't want to marry anyone. My parents did not give me a very entrancing view of the married state. They hated the sight of each other!'

She looked up in shock at that grated revelation. 'You never told me that!'

'You have so many illusions about happy family life, I could never bring myself to tell you the truth.' His dark gaze was unrelentingly grim. 'My parents married because they had to marry. My mother was pregnant. They didn't love each other. They didn't even like each other. They lived together all those years in absolute misery. And the only thing they ever wanted from me was money. As long as the money came, they hadn't the slightest interest in what I was doing. But it took me a long while to face that reality. When that plane went down, the only things I lost were a sister and two parents who never wanted to be parents in the first place.'

Shutting her eyes tightly, she lowered her head. 'I always thought your family loved you.'

'They loved what I could give them,' he contradicted fiercely. 'And you're not so very different, are you? Ten days ago, you were sitting in Huntingdon's apartment ready to marry him. Miraculously, you converted to me!'

'He asked me to marry him that day you saw us. There was never anything between us before that. At least not on my side. I should have been honest about that sooner,' she conceded uncertainly.

'Honest?' he gritted. 'You don't know the meaning of the word. I look forward to you telling my son in another few years that the reason for my late appearance in his life lies with your fear of my intentions towards him before he was even born!'

She flinched at the image he projected.

'What have you told him about me?'

She might as well have been hanging from a cliff by her fingernails. One by one, he was breaking them, loosening their hold, bringing the jagged rocks of retribution closer and closer. She chose to jump. 'Nothing,' she admitted shakily.

'Nothing?' he exclaimed. 'You must have told him something about his father!'

She broke into a faltering explanation of Harriet's cover-story. She could not have said that he absorbed the details. He zoomed in on only one, cutting her short in another surge of shuddering rage when he realised that Daniel thought his father was dead. The last straw had broken the camel's back. That Luc should not know he had had a son was bad enough. But that Daniel should not know about him was unforgivable.

She was desperately confused by what he had told her in anger, confidences which she sensed that in his present mood would never have been made otherwise. He had said that he loved her five years ago. All else receded before that single stated fact. The love she had longed

to awaken had been there. And she had been too blind
and too insecure to even suspect its existence for herself.

Why had she listened to Harriet? Why, oh, why? But
it wasn't fair to blame Harriet. Harriet had judged Luc
on the evidence of what Catherine herself had told her.
Harriet had influenced her only in so far as she had con-
firmed what Catherine had already believed. And Luc
had just brought down the convictions that had sustained her through the years like a pack of cards.

Enormous guilt weighted her now. She had run away
when she should have stood her ground, stayed away
when she should have returned. A little voice said that
what Luc said so impressively now with the benefit of
hindsight was no very good guide to how he might have
reacted to her pregnancy without having sustained the
shock of first losing her. That voice was quashed because the guilt was greater. Luc would have married her.
Daniel would have had a father. Daniel would have had
many things and many advantages which she had not
had the power to give him.

Luc was right on one count. She had not given him
a chance. In her own mind, the result had been a fore-
gone conclusion. Then, she had to admit, it had been
easier to run away than face a confrontation. In those
days, she had been out of her depth with Luc, unable
to hold her own. She could not have dreamt then that
Luc could be so bitter or indeed that losing her could
have brought him so much pain. For it had been pain
that powered that bitterness, that fierce conviction that
she had betrayed him for the second time. Luc viewed
her response to his lovemaking last night in the same
light as he had viewed that long-ago last night in New
York.

And she understood facets of his temperament which
she had not understood before. The heat in the bedroom,
the coolness beyond it. Recently he had begun to break
out of that pattern. But he must have learnt early in life

not to show his emotions. And he must have been hurt. His parents, by all accounts, had not encouraged or sought his affection. The financial generosity, which in the past had made her feel like an object to be bought, was shown now in a different light. Luc had had a long history before her of giving to those closest to him. It had been expected of him. When his family had died, he had simply continued the same habit with her.

There was so much fear trapped inside her. Luc was more than disappointed in her: Luc was embittered and disillusioned. Five years ago, whether she knew it or not, she had thumped the last nail into her coffin. It had never occurred to Luc that she might have been pregnant because it had equally never occurred to him that, if she was, she might go to such lengths to conceal the fact from him.

But what a disaster it would have been had Luc felt forced to marry her, repeating what he surely would have believed to be his parents' mistake. He had not been ready to make such a commitment of his own free will. It wouldn't have worked, it couldn't have worked, but Luc could not see that. No, at this moment Luc saw only Daniel, and he was already demonstrating a voracious appetite for knowledge of his son. He wanted Daniel. Right now, he did not want Daniel's mother.

Anger was within him still, anger dangerously encased in ice which could shatter again. When Luc came to terms with the awareness that he was a father, how would he feel about her then? He had trusted her. He had blamed himself entirely for her defection in the past. He had wanted to put the clock back, make everything right...she could see that now. And now he had learnt that that wasn't possible. It was very probable, she registered strickenly, that the driving determination of his to take what he wanted had resulted in a too hasty marriage.

'I love Daniel very much,' she murmured tightly.

'You have a fine way of showing it,' he censured. 'You dump him in the back of beyond with some seething feminist——'

'Don't you dare call Peggy that!' Catherine interrupted hotly. 'She's a university lecturer and she's written three books. She's also a very good friend.'

But possibly Peggy wouldn't be a friend any more in the midst of this nightmare that had erupted. Kept in the dark about Luc's identity, railroaded from her family home by Rafaella, and told goodness knew what, Peggy was sure to be furious as well.

Catherine's wedding present was an Elizabethan country house. It wasn't enormous, it wasn't ostentatious and it would have stolen her heart had she been in a less wretched mood...and had Rafaella not been emerging from the front entrance, wreathed in welcoming smiles...

'Not bad as a pressie, not bad at all.' Hands on her slim hips, Peggy scanned the house in the early-evening sunshine, her wryly admiring scrutiny glossing over manicured lawns, a stretch of woodland and the more distant glimmer of a small lake. 'Strewth, Catherine, it's incredibly hard not to be impressed by all this.'

Catherine glanced at her watch helplessly again.

Too observant to miss the betraying gesture, Peggy frowned. 'They'll show up again sooner or later. Stop worrying. Daniel will come round. It's my fault,' she sighed. 'I shouldn't have left him alone with Rafaella for a second. The woman's poisonous.'

Catherine thought back reluctantly to their arrival. Luc had gone straight to greet Rafaella. Catherine had no idea what had passed between them but the brunette had been smiling and laughing, switching on to the ultra-feminine mode she invariably employed around Luc. Then, with a pretty little speech about not wanting to intrude, she had climbed into her car, no doubt smugly aware that she was leaving bedlam in her wake between husband and wife...and mother and son.

Daniel had been sitting like a solemn little old man in one of the downstairs rooms. Her attempt to put her arms round him had been fiercely rejected. 'You tol' me my daddy was dead!' Daniel had condemned and, from that point on, the reunion had gone from bad to worse.

Rafaella had done her work well. Daniel might be a very clever child but his grasp of adult relationships was no greater than any other four-year-old's. He understood solely that his mother had lied to him. Hurt and confused, terribly nervous of meeting this father Rafaella had described in over-impressive terms, Daniel had taken the brunt of his conflicting emotions out on Catherine.

Luc had taken over the same second he chose to join them, crouching down on his son's diminutive level to engage his attention. 'I don't know anything about being a father,' he had confided cleverly. 'I'll probably make mistakes. You'll have to help me.'

'I don't want a daddy who bosses me around all the time,' Daniel had traded in a small voice, but quick as a flash with the return.

'I wouldn't either,' Luc had agreed smoothly.

'I'm not sure I want one,' Daniel had admitted less argumentatively.

'I can understand that, but I am very sure that I want you to be my son.'

'Have you got any other ones?' Daniel asked innocently.

'Only you. That is what makes you so special.'

Catherine had hovered like a third wheel, watching without great surprise as Daniel had responded to Luc. Luc had put in a performance of unsurpassed brilliance, quieting all of Daniel's fears. It had gone on for ages. A series of extremely subtle negotiations on Luc's side and of blossoming confidence and curiosity on Daniel's.

Luc hadn't moved too far, too fast. A mutual sizing-up had been taking place. After an hour, Daniel had been chattering confidingly, flattered by Luc's interest in him, relaxed and unthreatened by his manner. Clover had been mentioned. It had taken Luc precisely five seconds to recognise that the retrieval of an elderly donkey from an animal sanctuary would do much to cement his new relationship with his son. And never let it be said that Luc would look a gift horse or, in this case, a gift donkey in the mouth. A phone call had established that Clover was still in residence.

'I think we should go and get her now, don't you?' Luc had suggested with the innate cool of a master tactician, and Daniel had been so overcome with tears, excitement and gratitude that he had flung himself at Luc, breaking the no-physical-contact barrier he had until that moment rigidly observed.

They had departed before lunch. 'He's a beautiful child,' Luc had murmured, choosing then to notice Catherine for the first time since their arrival. 'And I am very proud that he is mine.'

She still wasn't sure whether that had been a compliment, a veiled apology, a mere acknowledgement of Daniel's attractions or a concealed criticism that he had had to wait this long to meet his own son.

'You should have gone with them,' Peggy told her.

'I wasn't invited. Anyway,' she sighed, 'I needed to talk to you. I thought you'd be furious over all that's happened.'

'Are you kidding? The last two days have been excitement all the way!' Peggy laughed. 'I was staggered when Rafaella showed me that picture of you with Luc at the airport and by that time the first reporter was ringing. Someone in the village must have tipped them off. Lots of people knew I was taking Daniel up to my parents' place. When I go back, I can bask in your reflected glory...'

'There's not a lot of it around at the moment. You'll catch a chill,' Catherine warned ruefully. 'When all of this comes out——'

'When all of what comes out? Don't exaggerate,' Peggy scolded. 'You lived with him, it broke down, and now you're married to him. You can't get a lot of scandalous mileage out of that. Daniel's his, end of story.'

'It's not that simple——'

'Neither was the amount of information you contrived to leave out when you once briefly discussed Daniel's father with me,' Peggy interposed. 'I've met him for about ten minutes now and I'm not sure I'm very much the wiser. Mind you, he has three virtues not to be sneezed at. One, he's generous. I won't add that he can afford to be. Two, he has to be the best-looking specimen I've ever seen live off a movie-screen. That's a sexist observation, Catherine, but, shamefully, that *was* my first reaction. Three, anyone capable of charming Daniel out of a tantrum that fast is worthy of respect.'

'Anything else?'

'When he breezed off with Daniel and left you behind like faithful Penelope, I found myself hoping that Clover would be in a more than usually anti-social state of mind when he has to get close and enthuse. I bet he's never been within twenty feet of a donkey before!'

That so matched Catherine's thoughts that she burst out laughing, but her amusement was short-lived. She sighed. 'If I hadn't lost my memory, I'd have had to tell him about Daniel last week. That wouldn't have been quite so bad.'

'If you ask me, and you won't, so I'll give it to you for free,' Peggy murmured, 'where Daniel's concerned, Luc got what he deserved. If he hadn't made you so insecure you'd have trusted him enough to tell him. And it strikes me that he's bright enough to work that one out for himself.'

If he *wants* to work it out, Catherine reflected unhappily. And nothing Luc had said earlier in the day had given her the impression that he intended to make that leap in tolerant understanding. She walked Peggy back to her car, both dreading and anticipating Luc's return.

Clover arrived first, as irascible as ever, snapping at the gardener, who was detailed to take her to the paddock. Catherine was interrupted in the midst of her thanks to the lady who ran the animal sanctuary and had taken the trouble to deliver Clover back, and was informed with an embarrassed smile that Luc had made a most handsome donation to the sanctuary. Ironically, that irritated her. Why were things always so easy for Luc?

He strolled in after ten with Daniel fast asleep in his arms. On the brink of demanding to know where they had been all day, she caught herself up. The cool challenge in Luc's gaze informed her that he was prepared for exactly that kind of response. Moving forward, she took Daniel from him instead. 'I'll put him to bed.'

She carted her exhausted son up to the bedroom where he had slept for the previous two nights. He stirred while she was undressing him, eyes flying open in sudden panic. 'Where's Daddy?'

'Downstairs.'

'I thought I dreamt him.' Daniel gave her a sleepy, beguiling smile. 'He doesn't know anything about kids but he knows a lot about computers,' he said forgivingly, submitting to a hug and winding his arms round her neck. 'I'm sorry I was bad.'

Her eyes stung. 'I'll forgive you this once.'

'Daddy s'plained everything. It's all his fault we got split up,' he whispered, drifting off again.

From the bottom of her heart, she thanked Luc for that at least. He had put Daniel's needs before his own anger, healing the breach between Catherine and her son before it could get any wider. As it could have done.

Catherine was well aware that, for the foreseeable future, Luc would occupy centre stage with Daniel. Luc had had the power to swerve him even further in that direction. But he hadn't used it.

She went down to the drawing-room. For all its size, it had a cosy aspect of comfort, decorated as it was with the faded country-house look she had always admired. The interior lacked a lived-in quality, though. The housekeeper, Mrs Stokes, had gone to considerable trouble with flower arrangements in empty spaces, but it was so obvious that nobody had lived here in years. Mrs Stokes had told her quite casually that Luc had never even spent a night below this roof before.

And he had bought this house for her, had scarcely come near it after the first few months. Luc had had faith in her, she registered painfully. Luc had been convinced that she would return. What she had forced him to face today was that she had not had a corresponding faith in him. She had asked for nothing, expected nothing and, not surprisingly, nothing was what she had received.

'Is he asleep?' Luc paused on the threshold, leashed vitality vibrating from his poised stance. His veiled dark gaze was completely unreadable.

She cleared her dry throat. 'He went out like a light. You must have tired him out. That doesn't often happen.'

Luc moved a fluid shoulder. 'He doesn't have enough stimulation. He was on his very best behaviour with me, but I suspect displays of temper such as I witnessed earlier are not infrequent.'

'He was upset,' she said defensively.

'He's an extremely bright child. He should start school as soon as possible.'

She paled in dismay. 'I don't want him sent away.'

Luc raised a brow. 'Did I suggest that? He does not have to board. Rome has an excellent school for gifted children. The opportunity to compete with equals would benefit Daniel.' He took a deep breath, cast an almost wary look at her, but she wasn't looking at him. Tight-mouthed, she was staring at the floor. 'He's a little old to be throwing tantrums. That surplus energy could be better employed.'

'You're very critical!' she snapped.

'That wasn't my intention. He's an infinitely more well-balanced child than I was at the same age, but he needs more to occupy him. Unless you plan to continue letting him educate himself from the television set.'

Catherine reddened fiercely but she didn't argue, uneasily conscious that he had some grounds for that comment. 'I did my best.'

'He's basically a very happy, very confident child. I think you did a marvellous job, considering that you were on your own and, as Daniel assured me repeatedly, very short of money.'

The compliment only increased her tension. Luc was so distant, so controlled. She didn't recognise him like this. He was unnerving her. She stole a covert under-the-lashes glance at the vibrancy of his dark golden features, desperate to know how he felt now that he had had time to cool down.

'Was what you said to me this morning true? Or a fabrication of the moment?' he prompted very quietly. 'Did you really believe that I would have demanded that you have an abortion?'

The colour drained from her complexion. 'Put like that, it sounds so——'

'Cruel? Inhuman? Selfish?' he suggested, his beautiful eyes running like flames of dancing gold over her distressed face. 'Presumably that is how you saw me then.'

In bewilderment she shook her head at this incorrect assertion. 'I didn't . . . when something gets in your way, you get rid of it,' she stumbled, conscious that she was not expressing herself very well. 'I just felt that if that was what you wanted, I mightn't have been able to stand up to you. That was what I was most afraid of. I might have let you persuade me...'

Every angle of his strong bone-structure was whip-taut. '*Per amor di Dio*, what did I do to give you such an image of me?'

The scene wasn't working in the way she had hoped it would. Luc was dwelling with dangerously precise intensity on the jumbled mess of imprecise emotions and fears which had guided her almost five years ago. 'It wasn't like that. Can't you understand that the longer I kept quiet about it, the harder it was for me to tell you?'

'What I understand is that you were very much afraid of me and that you were convinced that I would kill my unborn child for convenience. Yet even when I didn't know that I loved you, I cared for you,' he murmured with flat emphasis. 'And even if I hadn't loved you, I still couldn't have chosen such a course of action.'

Tears lashed the back of her eyes. She blinked rapidly. 'I'm sorry.' It was a cry from the heart.

A grim curve hardened his mouth. 'I think it is I who should be sorry. I appear to have reaped what I sowed. And you had no more faith in me yesterday when you married me. You still couldn't summon up the courage to tell me about Daniel.'

'I'm a frightful coward... you ought to know that by now.' It was an uneasy joke that was truth. 'And anyway, I didn't want to spoil the wedding,' she muttered, not looking at him, too aware that it was a pathetic excuse.

The silence stretched, dragging her nerves unbearably tight.

'How much of a chance is there that this last week will threaten to extend the family circle?' he asked tautly.

As his meaning sank in, she licked her dry lips nervously, conscious that she would very soon have confirmation one way or another. 'Very little chance,' she proffered honestly, strangely, ridiculously embarrassed all of a sudden by the subject. Luc's attitude was a far cry from his attitude that day at the pool, and that day seemed so long ago now.

If he wasn't quite tactless enough to heave a loud sigh of relief at the news, he wasn't capable of concealing that she had alleviated a fairly sizeable apprehension. The most obvious aspects of his strong tension dissolved. 'I want you to know that I didn't think of repercussions either those first few days that we were together. I am not that unscrupulous,' he asserted, even managing a faint smile. 'I didn't plan to make you pregnant.'

'That's OK.' Catherine gave a jerky shrug, couldn't have got another word out, she was so desperately hurt by his reaction. The idea of another child had taken surprising root, she discovered belatedly. She saw Luc's withdrawal of enthusiasm as the ultimate rejection. It was only a tiny step further to the belief that he no longer saw their marriage as a permanent fixture. A second child would only have complicated matters.

'I was very careless,' he remarked.

Catherine wasn't listening to him. She was on the edge of bursting into floods of tears and bitter recriminations. A strategic retreat was called for. She cut a wide passage round him. 'I'm tired. I'm going to bed.'

'I won't disturb you.'

It was no consolation at all to discover that Luc's possessions had been removed from the main bedroom at some stage of the evening. He hadn't even given her the chance to throw him out! Grabbing a pillow, she punched it and then thrust her face in it to muffle her sobs.

CHAPTER TEN

'CAN I get you anything else, Mrs Santini?'

Catherine surveyed her plate guiltily. One croissant, shredded into about fifteen pieces, not a toothmark on one of them. 'No, thanks.' She forced a smile. 'I'm not very hungry.'

Her appetite was no more resilient than her heart. Luc had taken Daniel to Paris with him very early this morning. They would be back by evening. In Daniel's hearing, Luc had smoothly suggested that she might like to accompany them. Her refusal had been equally smoothly accepted. The invitation had clearly been for Daniel's benefit alone.

The past four days, she conceded numbly, had been hell upon earth. She had learnt the trick of shortening them. She went to bed early and slept late. Yet she could not fault Luc's behaviour. He was being scrupulously polite and considerate. Indeed, he was making a very special effort. It didn't come naturally to him. She could feel the raw tension behind the cool front. She could taste it in the air. He couldn't hide it from her.

He didn't love her. How could she ever have been foolish enough to believe that he might? Then again, she had a talent for dreaming, for believing what she wanted to believe, she conceded with bitter self-contempt. Luc had chased an illusion for almost five years and he had suddenly woken up to the truth. Daniel had been the catalyst, but even if Daniel hadn't existed Luc would inevitably have realised that he had made a mistake.

In her absence, Luc must have built her up to be something more exciting than she was. When he'd found her again, her reluctance and the challenge of apparently taking her away from another man had provoked that dark, savage temperament of his. All that mattered to him was winning. Having won, he'd found that the battle had not proved to be worth the prize.

He was in a quandary now. It would look exceedingly strange if their marriage broke up too soon. There was also Daniel to be considered. At least, however, there would be no other child. She sat rigidly in the dining chair, a tempest of emotion storming through her slight body.

She was not carrying his child. The proof had come that very night when she had abandoned herself to grief. There would be no other baby, no further tie by which she might hold him. Her sane mind told her that was fortunate, but more basic promptings rebelled against that cooler judgement.

She could not picture life without Luc again. That terrified her. The more distant he was, the more desperate she felt. She couldn't eat, she couldn't sleep, she couldn't do anything. What was there now? she asked herself. What had he left her? Daniel adored him. Daniel could hardly bear Luc out of his sight.

Her future stretched emptily before her. Daniel would start school in Rome. Initially she would be there as well but, little by little, the marriage that had never quite got off the ground would shift into a separation. Luc would make lengthy business trips and she would no doubt do what was expected of her and make regular visits back to England. Certainly it would be impossible for her to withstand continual exposure to Luc as he was now.

It was torture to be so close and yet so far, to shake with wanting him in the loneliness of her bed at night, to exhaust herself by day keeping up a pretence that she was quite happy with things as they were. Damp-eyed, she lifted her head high. She would not let Luc see how much he was hurting her. Pride demanded that she equal his detachment and make no attempt to break it.

Not that she thought she was managing to be totally convincing. In between all the pleases and thank-yous she had never heard so many of before, she occasionally encountered searching stares. His tension spoke for itself. Luc wanted her to let go with finesse. He was willing her not to force some melodramatic scene. Rage and despair constrained her in an iron yoke of silence, creating an inner conflict that threatened to tear her apart. Why couldn't he have left her alone? Why had he had to thrust his way back into her life? Why had he laid a white rose on her pillow? Why had he had to force her to admit that, far from hating him, she loved him? Why? Why? Why?

Angered by her own desperation, she stood up, determined not to spend another day wandering about like a lost soul. For starters, it was time she saw Drew, time she stopped avoiding that issue. After all, she had already contacted his godmother. Mrs Anstey had ranted down the phone at her, refusing her apologies and telling her with satisfaction that she had given the flat to a great-niece, who would be far more suitable. Catherine had taken the verbal trouncing in silence. It had lightened her conscience.

She didn't expect her meeting with Drew to be quite so straightforward. Did she tell him that she was responsible for the nerve-racking experiences he must have endured in Germany? Or did he already know? Would he even want to see her now?

It was early afternoon when she entered the compact offices that housed Huntingdon Components. Drew's secretary phoned through an announcement of her arrival. Drew emerged from his office, his pleasant features stiff and almost expressionless. 'This is a surprise.'

'I felt I had to see you.'

'I'm afraid I don't know quite how to greet Mrs Luc Santini.'

She tilted her chin. 'I'm still Catherine,' she murmured steadily.

He stood at the window, his back half turned to her. 'I tried to call you from Germany. My housekeeper told me that you'd cleared out without even staying the night. She said the bedroom was so tidy that she wasn't too sure you'd been in it at all.'

Catherine bent her head. Luc's security staff were thorough.

'Then I saw that photo of you at the airport with Santini. It was in every newspaper,' he sighed. 'Daniel is the image of him. Harriet lied about your background. I put that together for myself.'

'I'm sorry that I couldn't tell you the truth.'

'It was none of my business when I first knew you. But I preferred competing with a ghost,' he admitted wryly, and hesitated. 'To take off with him like that, you have to be crazy about him...'

Her vague idea of explaining what had really happened died there. Somehow she felt it would be disloyal to Luc. Drew had no need of that information. 'Yes,' she agreed, half under her breath, and then, looking up, asked, 'Did you get your contract?'

Unexpectedly, he smiled widely. 'Not the one I went out for. Quite coincidentally, an even more promising prospect came up. It's secured the firm's future for a long time to come. What's that saying? Lucky at cards, unlucky in love?'

Her eyes clouded over, but she was shaken to realise that Drew was quite unaware that his firm had been under threat and had ultimately profited from the change in contracts. He had undergone no anxiety, and the news that he had achieved that second contract through Luc's influence would not be welcome.

He cleared his throat awkwardly. 'I've agreed to go to counselling with Annette, but I don't know if it will change anything.'

A smile chased the tension from her soft mouth. 'I'm glad,' she said sincerely.

'I still think you're pure gold, Catherine.' His mouth twisted. 'I just hope that he appreciates how lucky he is.'

Not so's you'd notice, she repined helplessly as she climbed back into the limousine. A male, punch-drunk on his good fortune, did not willingly vacate the marital bed and avoid all physical contact. Quite obviously, Luc couldn't bring himself to touch her. The white-hot heat of his hunger had died along with the illusion. But it hadn't died for her. Her love had never been an illusion. She had never been blind to Luc's flaws or her own. She still ached with wanting him. And soon she would despise herself again for that weakness.

It was wrong to let Luc do this to her. It was undignified, degrading...cowardly. Their marriage had been a mistake. Continuing it purely for the sake of appearances demanded too high a cost of her self-respect. Nor could she sacrifice herself for Daniel's sake. Daniel was like Luc. Daniel would survive. It was her own survival that was at risk. She couldn't afford to sit back and let events overtake her as she had done so often in the past. A clean break was the only answer and it was for her to take the initiative.

Dazed by the acknowledgement, she wandered round Harrods in the afternoon. The heavens were falling on her. The ground was suddenly rocking beneath her feet. It was over...over. She had felt this way once before and she had never wanted to feel like this again.

The chauffeur was replacing the phone when she returned to the car. 'Mr Santini's back from Paris, madam. I said we'd be back within two hours, allowing for the traffic.'

Dear heaven, for someone who didn't give two hoots about her, Luc certainly kept tabs on her! She was suddenly very reluctant to go home. It would be better, she reasoned, if Daniel was in bed when she returned.

'We'll be later,' she said. 'I want to stop somewhere for a meal.'

She selected a hotel. She spent ages choosing from the chef's recommendations, chasing each course round the plate and deciding what she would say to Luc, how she would say it and, more importantly, how she would look when she said it. Cool, calm and collected. Not martyred, not distressed, not apologetic. When she told Luc that she wanted an immediate separation, she would do it with dignity.

She was tiptoeing up the stairs, deciding that she would feel fresher and more dignified in the morning, when Luc strode out of the drawing-room. 'Where the hell have you been?' he demanded, making her jump with fright.

'Out.' Carefully not sparing his lean, dark physique a single visually disturbing glance, she murmured, 'I want a separation, Luc.'

'Prego?' It was very faint. She studied him then, unable to resist the temptation. The lights above shed cruel clarity on the sudden pallor defining his hard bone-structure. For some reason, he looked absolutely shattered by her announcement. It also occurred to her that he had lost weight over the last few days.

'We can talk about it tomorrow.' Consumed by raging misery, she lost heart in her prepared speeches about incompatability.

'We talk about it now. You've been with Huntingdon!' The condemnation came slamming back at her with ferocious bite as he mounted the stairs two at time.

He was seething, she registered bemusedly.

'You go slinking back to him the instant my back's turned. I won't let you go,' he swore fiercely. 'I'll kill him if he comes near you!'

'I can't think why. After all——'

'After all *nothing*,' he cut in wrathfully. 'You're my wife.'

Gingerly, she pressed open her bedroom door. 'Your room's next door, I seem to recall,' she reminded him for want of anything better to say.

'I was a fool to take that lying down! How dare you put me out of your bed?' he ground out between clenched white teeth, following her in, slamming the door with a resounding crash.

She blinked. 'I didn't——'

'I should never have stood for it. You played on my guilt!'

Catherine was frowning. 'Mrs Stokes must have moved your luggage. I remember her asking me how many bedrooms Castelleone had. We talked a lot about bedrooms but I really wasn't paying much attention——'

'Is this a private conversation or can anyone join in? I don't know what you're talking about!'

'She must have realised we had separate bedrooms in Italy and she probably assumed we wanted the same set-up here.' She smiled at him sunnily. 'You thought I was responsible?'

A dark flush had risen over his cheekbones. 'I came in very quietly and you were asleep that night. My clothes had gone.'

'I thought you'd told her to move them.' She could hardly credit that a mistake on the housekeeper's part had led to such a misunderstanding. 'Why didn't you say something?'

He looked ever so slightly sheepish. 'I didn't know what to say. All that day I was in shock at what you said to me on the jet.' He shifted a beautifully shaped brown hand in a movement of frustration. 'It only happens with you,' he breathed tautly.

She watched him move fluidly across the room like a restive cat night-prowling on velvet paws. 'What only happens with me?'

His jawline clenched. 'I lose my temper and I say things I don't mean.' Long fingers balled into a fist and then vanished into the pocket of his well-cut trousers. Discomfiture was written all over him. 'But that you should distrust me to such an extent...it...it hurt.'

So did saying it. She longed to reach out and put her arms round him, but sensed how unwelcome it would be. He was so proud, so defensive and ill-at-ease with words that came so easily to her. He was fluent in every other mood but this one, where deeper emotions intruded. And he was only talking now because anger had spurred him to the attempt.

'I was very insecure when I was pregnant,' she said uncertainly. 'You were breaking me up, Luc. Emotionally I was in a mess. I just didn't have the courage to face you with a complication you didn't want. It never occurred to me that you might choose to insist on marrying me or want to take any responsibility for the child I was expecting...'

The muscles in his strong brown throat worked. 'You don't have to justify your decision. I don't blame you for what you did,' he said almost indistinctly. 'I had to lose you before I could appreciate what you meant to me.'

He hadn't vacated the marital bed. He understood what she had done five years ago. He wasn't holding it against her as if she had failed him. He was accepting that, whether he liked it or not, it had been inevitable.

'Actually, if I hadn't been hit by that car,' she muttered, 'I would have phoned you.'

He paled. 'What car?'

She told him about the accident in the car park and the months she had spent in hospital. He was visibly appalled and shaken, but he didn't take her into his arms as she had secretly hoped. He wandered over to the window and looked back at her with glittering dark eyes. 'The first time I saw you, you reminded me of a Christmas-tree angel. Very fragile, not intended for human handling. You were wearing a hideous dress covered with roses and you were so tiny, it wore you. When I smiled at you you lit up like an electric light and you chattered non-stop for fifteen solid minutes,' he extended very quietly. 'You got lost in the middle of sentences. You didn't hear the phone ringing. You didn't notice that a woman came in and walked round while I was there. You were so dizzy, you fascinated me. I'd never met anyone like you before. You want to hear that I was ravished at first glance but I wasn't.'

'I never thought you were.' Her cheeks were hot enough to light a fire.

'That night I didn't think of you in a sexual way,' he was scrupulously careful to tell her.

'Nostalgia's not your thing,' she muttered fiercely.

'But I'd met anyone with so much natural warmth. Being with you was like standing in the sunshine. When I walked away, I felt as though I'd kicked a puppy...'

Her nails ploughed furrows into her palms.

'It was surprisingly hard to walk away,' he confided in an undertone. 'Over the next two months, you kept drifting into my mind at the oddest times. I slept with another woman and then I would think about you. It was infuriating.'

'I'm not overcome by it either!' she snapped.

'When I was next in London, I didn't intend to look you up again. In fact, I had a woman with me on that trip. I deliberately went to a different hotel that was nowhere near the gallery.'

'Am I supposed to *want* to hear this?'

Tense dark eyes flickered over her and veiled. 'I never slept with her. She got on my nerves and I sent her back to New York. I was callous about it. I was callous in most of my dealings with women in those days. But I found I couldn't be callous with you. You had incredible pulling-power, *cara*. I was back at the gallery the second she left for the airport.'

'Why?' Involuntarily, she was finding that this was compulsive listening, a window on to a once blank wall.

'I didn't know why then. You were so extravagantly pleased to see me, it was as though you'd been waiting for me. Or as though you knew something I didn't. And perhaps you did.' An almost tender smile softened his mouth. 'It was unsettling. It threw me. I haven't asked a woman to go for a walk since I was thirteen. I was in a foul mood and you talked me out of it. You were so painfully honest about yourself and so agonisingly young, but somehow...' he hesitated '...you made me feel ten feet tall.'

'I made you feel so good it took you another two months to show up again!' she protested.

He released his breath in a hiss. 'You were only eighteen. You didn't belong in my world. I didn't want to hurt you. I also never wanted to make love to anyone as badly as I wanted you that night. I was twenty-seven, but I felt like a middle-aged lecher!' he gritted abruptly. 'I didn't plan to see you ever again.'

'Have you any idea how many nights I sat up, waiting for you to call?'

'I knew it.' He sounded grimly fatalistic. 'I could feel you waiting and I couldn't get you out of my head. I also found that I couldn't stay away from you. I believed that once I went to bed with you I would be cured.'

'That's disgusting!' she gasped.

'*Per Dio*, what do you want? The truth or a fairy-tale?' he slashed back at her in sudden anger. 'You think it is easy for me to admit these things? The lies I told to myself? That first night in Switzerland—how is it you describe euphoria? You thought you'd died and gone to heaven? Well, so did I, the first time I made love to you!'

The shocked line of her mouth had softened into a faint smile.

'But naturally I assured myself that I only felt that way because it was the best sex I'd ever had.'

Her smile evaporated like Scotch mist.

'I was in love with you but I didn't want to accept that fact,' he admitted harshly. 'I hated being away from you but I didn't want to take you abroad with me. The papers would have got hold of you then.'

'Would that have mattered?'

'Seven years ago, *cara*, you couldn't have handled a more public place in my life.' He shrugged in a jerky motion. 'And I didn't want to share you with anyone. I didn't want other women bitching at you. I didn't want gossip columnists cheapening what we had.'

She lowered her head. 'And perhaps you didn't want anyone realising that I had a literacy problem.'

'Yes. That both embarrassed and angered me.' He had to force out the admission. 'But I wouldn't have felt like that had I known you were dyslexic. I could have been open about that. In spite of that, wherever you were was home for me. If something worried me, I forgot about it when I was with you. I didn't realise until you had gone just how much I relied on you.'

She was trying very hard not to cry. He pulled her rigid figure into his arms very slowly, very gently. 'I have few excuses for what I did five years ago. But, if it is any consolation to you, I paid; *Dio . . .*' he said feelingly, 'I paid for not valuing you as I should have done. If only I'd intercepted you before you left the apartment that morning! I must have missed you by no more than an hour.'

She bowed her head against his broad chest, drowning in the warm masculine scent of him, feeling weak, shivery and on the brink of melting. 'I hated leaving you.'

'For a while, *bella mia*, I too hated you for leaving.' The hand smoothing through her hair was achingly gentle. 'It was the one and only time I lost interest in making money. I hit the bottle pretty hard...'

She was shocked. 'You?'

'Me. I felt unbelievably sorry for myself. I let everything slide.'

Her brow indented. 'Drew told me that you almost lost the shirt off your back a few years ago. Was that true?'

'It was.'

'Over me?' she whispered incredulously.

'I needed you,' he said gruffly. 'I missed you. I felt very alone.'

Tears swimming in her eyes, she wrapped her arms tightly round him, too upset by the image he invoked to speak.

'I picked myself up again because I believed you would come back,' he shared. 'When I saw you in the Savoy two weeks ago there was nothing I would not have done to get you back.'

'No?' She positively glowed at the news.

'It was not, however, how I pictured our reconciliation. You shouldn't have been with another man. You should have looked pleased to see me, instead of horror-stricken. I'm afraid I went off the rails that day,' he breathed tautly.

'Did you?' She smiled up at him, unconcerned.

He frowned down at her. 'I threatened you. I took advantage of your amnesia to practically kidnap you. You could have been madly in love with Huntingdon and I was determined that you would get over it. When you came round in the clinic and smiled at me, I was lost to all conscience. When I realised you'd lost your memory, all I could think about was getting you out of the country.'

'You were always quick to recognise a good opportunity,' she sighed approvingly.

Long fingers cupped her cheekbones. 'Catherine, what I did was wrong. This week, after I learnt about Daniel and cooled down, which I did very quickly, I felt very ashamed of what I had done. It was completely unscrupulous of me.'

'If you say so.' She wound her arms round his neck, stretching up on tiptoe. 'Personally I think it was thrilling. I waited twenty-four and a half years to be spirited off to an Italian castle, and I wouldn't have missed it for the world.'

'Be serious.' He was alarmingly set on contrition. In fact, the more forgiving she became, the more grim he looked. 'Be honest with me. Can you forgive me for what I have said and done?'

'I forgive you freely, absolutely and forever. Do you want to know why?' she whispered teasingly. 'You're crazy about me...aren't you?' She drew back to stare up at him, suffering a sudden lurch in overwhelming confidence.

Brilliant golden eyes shimmered almost fiercely over her anxious face. 'Only a lunatic would behave the way I did if I wasn't,' he grated. 'Of course I love you!'

'I don't want a separation...I don't even want a separate bedroom,' she swore.

'Relax—you weren't getting either. What I have, I hold.' He lifted her with wonderful ease off her feet. 'But I should never have made love to you before you regained your memory. Unfortunately that night I found you in my bed,' his voice thickened betrayingly, 'I could not resist you.'

'I can't resist you, either.' She sank small determined hands into his black hair and drew his mouth down to hers. He lowered her to the bed without breaking the connection. It was some minutes before she remembered to breathe again.

'It's been torture to stay away from you,' he admitted roughly. 'But I believed that was what you wanted. I went to all that trouble arranging to go to Paris, thinking that you would be tempted to come, and you said no.'

'Serves you right for being so casual about it.'

He shuddered beneath the caressing sweep of her hands. 'Don't do that,' he groaned, pinning her provocative hands to the mattress. 'When you do that, I react like a teenager.'

'Why do you think I do it?' she murmured wickedly.

'*Dio*, I want you so much,' he said raggedly, removing her dress with more speed than expertise. Abruptly he stopped dead, staring down at her. 'It isn't safe, is it? I could make you pregnant.'

'The best things in life are dangerous. It's your choice,' she whispered.

'You wouldn't mind?' He looked dazed. 'By the pool that day, you weren't very enthusiastic about the idea. That's why I worried that it was too late.'

She ran a loving fingertip across his sensual mouth. 'I'm afraid all those intensely erotic experiences in Italy were unproductive.'

He nipped at her fingertip with his teeth, a brilliant smile curving his lips. 'Give me a month's trial.'

'You're so modest.' She blushed under raking golden eyes, heat striking her to the very centre of her body, making her tremble deliciously. He started to kiss her slowly and deeply and hungrily until conversation was the last thing on either of their minds.

What followed was wild, passionate and incredibly sweet. And afterwards he told her how much he loved her in Italian and English and French.

'You've got a certain *je ne sais quoi*,' Catherine conceded against a damp brown shoulder, letting the tip of her tongue slide teasingly across his smooth skin.

Luc's tousled dark head lifted, a sudden lancing grin flashing across his darkly handsome features. 'I understood that I was a habit.'

'You are,' she sighed with a voluptuous little wriggle of glorious contentment. 'An addictive one. Didn't I mention that?'

HARLEQUIN ✦ PRESENTS®

A Year
DOWN UNDER

In 1993, Harlequin Presents celebrates the land down
under. In June, let us take you to the Australian Outback,
in OUTBACK MAN by Miranda Lee,
Harlequin Presents #1562.

Surviving a plane crash in the Australian Outback is
surely enough trauma to endure. So why does Adrianna
have to be rescued by Bryce McLean, a man so gorgeous
that he turns all her cherished beliefs upside-down? But
the desert proves to be an intimate and seductive setting
and suddenly Adrianna's only realities are the red-hot
dust *and* Bryce....

Share the adventure—and the romance—
of A Year Down Under!

Available this month in
A YEAR DOWN UNDER

SECRET ADMIRER
by Susan Napier
Harlequin Presents #1554
Wherever Harlequin books are sold.

YDU-MY

Take 4 bestselling love stories FREE

Plus get a FREE surprise gift!

Special Limited-time Offer

Mail to Harlequin Reader Service®

P. O. Box 609
Fort Erie, Ontario
L2A 5X3

YES! Please send me 4 free Harlequin Presents® novels and my free surprise gift. Then send me 6 brand-new novels every month, which I will receive months before they appear in bookstores. Bill me at the low price of $2.49 each—plus 25¢ delivery and GST*. That's the complete price and compared to the cover prices of $2.89 each—quite a bargain! I understand that accepting the books and gift places me under no obligation ever to buy any books. I can always return a shipment and cancel at any time. Even if I never buy another book from Harlequin, the 4 free books and the surprise gift are mine to keep forever.

306 BPA AJJT

Name _____ (PLEASE PRINT)

Address _____ Apt. No. _____

City _____ Province _____ Postal Code _____

This offer is limited to one order per household and not valid to present Harlequin Presents® subscribers.
*Terms and prices are subject to change without notice.
Canadian residents will be charged applicable provincial taxes and GST.

CPRES-93R   ©1990 Harlequin Enterprises Limited

Where do you find hot Texas nights, smooth Texas charm,
and dangerously sexy cowboys?

WHITE LIGHTNING

by Sharon Brondos

Back a winner—Texas style!

Lynn McKinney knows Lightning is a winner and she is
totally committed to his training, despite her feud with her
investors. All she needs is time to prove she's right. But
once business partner Dr. Sam Townsend arrives on the
scene, Lynn realizes time is about to run out!

CRYSTAL CREEK reverberates with the exciting rhythm of
Texas. Each story features the rugged individuals who live
and love in the Lone Star State. And each one ends with
the same invitation...

Y'ALL COME BACK...REAL SOON!

**Don't miss WHITE LIGHTNING by Sharon Brondos.
Available in June wherever Harlequin books are sold.**